William Clark Russell

The Honour of the Flag

William Clark Russell

The Honour of the Flag

ISBN/EAN: 9783337079987

Printed in Europe, USA, Canada, Australia, Japan

Cover: Foto ©Andreas Hilbeck / pixelio.de

More available books at **www.hansebooks.com**

THE HONOUR OF
THE FLAG

BY

W. CLARK RUSSELL

AUTHOR OF "THE WRECK OF THE GROSVENOR,"
"LIFE OF LORD NELSON," ETC., ETC.

G. P. PUTNAM'S SONS

NEW YORK   LONDON
27 West Twenty-third Street   24 Bedford Street, Strand

The Knickerbocker Press

1895

The Knickerbocker Press, New Rochelle, N. Y.

Contents.

I

The Honour of the Flag.

A THAMES TRAGEDY.

MANIFOLD are the historic interests of the river Thames. There is scarcely a foot of its mud from London Bridge to Gravesend Reach that is not as "consecrated" as that famous bit of soil which Dr. Samuel Johnson and Mr. Richard Savage knelt and kissed on stepping ashore at Greenwich. One of the historic interests, however, threatens to perish out of the annals. It does not indeed rise to such heroic proportions as you find in the story of the Dutch invasion of the river, or in old Hackluyt's solemn narrative of the sailing of the expedition organised by Bristol's noble worthy, Sebastian Cabot ; but it is altogether too good and stirring to merit erasure from the Thames's history books by the neglect or ignorance of the historian.

3

It is absolutely true : I pledge my word for that on the authority of the records of the Whitechapel County Court.

In the year 1851 there dwelt on the banks of the river Thames a retired tailor, whom I will call John Sloper, out of regard to the feelings of his posterity, if such there be. This man had for many years carried on a flourishing trade in the east end of London. Having got together as much money as he might suppose would supply his daily needs, he built himself a villa near the pleasant little town of Erith. His house overlooked the water ; in front of it sloped a considerable piece of garden ground.

Mr. Sloper showed good sense and good taste in building himself a little home on the banks of the Thames. All day long he was able, if he pleased, to entertain himself with the sight of as stirring and striking a marine picture as is anywhere to be witnessed. He could have built himself a house above bridges, where there is no lack of elegance and river beauty of many sorts ; but he chose to command a view of the Thames on its commercial side.

In his day there was more life in the river than there is now. In our age

the great steamer thrusts past and is
quickly gone ; the tug runs the sail-
ing-ship to the docks or to her moor-
ing buoys, and there is no life in the
fabric she drags.   In Sloper's time
steamers were few ; the water of the
river teemed with sailing craft of
every description ; they tacked across
from bank to bank as they staggered
to their destination against the wind.

Sloper, sitting at his open window
on a fine day, would be able to count
twenty different types of rigs in almost as many minutes. That he
took a keen interest in ships, however, I do not assert; that he could
have told you the difference between
a brig and a schooner is barely imagi-
nable. The board on which Sloper
had flourished was not shipboard, it
had nothing to do with starboard or
larboard ; he was a tailor, not a
sailor, and the friends who ran down
to see him were of his own sort and
condition.

Sloper was a widower ; how many
years he had lived with his wife I
can't say. She died one Easter Monday, and when Sloper took possession
of his new house near Erith he
mounted some small cannon on his
lawn, and these pieces of artillery he
regularly fired every Easter Monday
in celebration of what he called the

joyfullest anniversary of his life. From which it is to be assumed that Sloper and his wife had not lived together very happily. But though the Whitechapel County Court records have been searched and inquiries made in that part of London where Sloper's shop was situated, it has not been discovered that Mrs. Sloper's end was hastened by her husband's cruelty ; that, in short, more happened between them than constant quarrels. Yet it must be said that Sloper behaved as though, in truth (as the old adage would put it), his little figure contained no more than the ninth part of a soul, when he mounted his guns and rudely and noisily triumphed over the dead whom he perhaps might have been afraid of in life, and coarsely emphasised with blasts of gunpowder his annual joy over his release.

Now in the east end of London, not above twenty minutes' walk from Sloper's old shop, there lived a sailor, named Joseph Westlake. This man had served when a boy under Collingwood, had smelt gunpowder at Navarino under Codrington, had been concerned in several dashing cutting-out jobs in the West Indies, and was altogether as hearty and worthy a specimen of an old English sailor of

the vanished school as you could ask
to see.

He had been shot in the leg ; he
carried a great scar over his brow ;
he was as full of yarns as a piece of
ancient ship's biscuit of weevils ; he
swore with more oaths than a Dutchman ; sneered prodigiously at steam ;
and held the meanest opinion of the
then existing race of seamen, who,
he said, never could have won the
old battles which had been the making of this kingdom, whether under
Howe's or gallant Jervis's, or the
lion-hearted Nelson's flag.

The country had no further need
of his services on his being paid off
out of his last ship, and he was somewhat at a loss, until happening to be
in the neighbourhood of Wapping,
and looking in upon an old shipmate
who kept a public house, he learnt
that a lawyer had been making inquiries for him.   He called upon that
lawyer, and was astounded to hear
that during his absence from England
a fortune of £15,000 had been left to
him by an aunt in Australia.

Joe Westlake on this took a little
house in the Stepney district, and endeavoured to settle down as an east-
end gent ; but his efforts to ride to a
shore-going anchor were hopeless.
His mind was always roaming.   He

had followed the sea man and boy for hard upon fifty years, and the cry of his heart was still for water — water without rum !—water fresh or salt ! it mattered not what sort of water it was so long as it *was*—water.

So as Joe Westlake found that he could n't rest ashore he looked about him, and, after a while, fell in with and purchased a smart little cutter, which he re-christened the *Tom Bowling*, out of admiration of the song which no sailor ever sang more sweetly than he. It was perfectly consistent with his traditions as a man-of-warsman that, having bought his little ship, he should arm her. He equipped her with four small carronades and a pivoted brass six-pounder on the forecastle. He then went to work to man her, but he did not very easily find a crew. Joe was fastidious in his ideas of seamen, and though some whom he cast his eye upon came very near to his taste, it cost him a great deal of trouble to discover the particular set of Jacks he wanted.

Three at last he found : Peter Plum, Bob Robins, and Tom Tuck. Joe was admiral ; Plum, coming next, combined a number of grades. He was captain, first lieutenant, and boatswain. Robins was the ship's working company, and Tom Tuck cooked and was the all-round handy man of the *Tom Bowling*.

It was Mr. Joe Westlake's intention to live on board his cutter; he furnished his cabin plainly and comfortably, and laid in a plentiful stock of liquor and tobacco. As he was to cruise under his own flag, and was indeed an admiral on his own account, he conferred with his first lieutenant, Peter Plum, on the question of a colour : what description of flag should he fly at his masthead ? They both started with the understanding that nothing under a fathom and a half in length was worth hoisting. After much discussion it was agreed that the device should consist of a very small jack in the top corner, and in the middle a crown with a wooden leg under it—the timber toe being in both Westlake's and Plum's opinion the most pregnant symbol of Britannia's greatness that the imagination could devise.

Within a few months of his landing from the frigate out of which he had been paid, Mr. Joseph Westlake was again afloat, but now in a smart little vessel of his own. She had been newly sheathed with copper, and when she heeled over from the breeze as she stretched through the winding reaches of the river the metal shone like gold above the wool-white line of foam through which the cutter washed, and lazy men in barges would turn their heads to admire her, and red-capped cooks in the cabooses of "ratching" colliers would step to the rail to look, and sometimes a party of gay and gallant Cockneys, male and female, taking their pleasure in a wherry, would salute the passing *Tom Bowling* with a flourish of hands and pocket-handkerchiefs.

Never had old Joe been so happy in all his life. Of a night he 'd bring up in some secure nook, and after having seen everything all safe, he 'd go below with Peter Plum, and in the cosy interior of the little cabin, whose atmosphere was rendered speedily fragrant with the perfume of rum punch, which Joe, whilst in the West Indies, had learnt the art of brewing to perfection, the two sailors would sit smoking their yards of pipe-clay whilst they discoursed on the past, one incident recalling another, one briny recollection prompting an even salter memory, until their eyes grew moist and their vision dim in their balls of sight; whereupon they would turn in and make the little ship vocal with their noses.

It happened, according to the usual methods of time, that an Easter Monday came round, which, as we know, was the joyful anniversary of the death of the wife of the retired tailor, Sloper, whose villa, called Labour's Retreat, stood upon the banks of the Thames near Erith. To fitly celebrate this happy day Mr. Sloper had invited three friends to dine with him. It was in the year 1851, when the class of society in which Mr. Sloper belonged was not so genteel in its habits as it has since become; in other words, Sloper dined at two o'clock. Had he survived into this age he would not have dreamt of dining at an earlier hour than seven.

His friends were of his own sex. Sloper did not like the ladies. His friends' calling matters not. They did business in the east end of London, and were all three thoroughly respectable tradesmen in a small way, wanting, perhaps, in the muscle and depth of chest and hurricane lungs of Joe Westlake and Peter Plum, but all of them able to pay twenty shillings in the pound, to give good value for prompt cash, and desirous not only of fresh patronage, but determined to a man to merit the continuance of the same.

When Sloper and his friends had

dined, and the bottle had circled until, like quicksilver in the eye of a
hurricane, the contents had sunk out
of sight, the party went on to the
lawn to fire off the guns there in com-
pletion of the triumphant celebration
of the ever-memorable anniversary of
Sloper's release.

It was precisely at this hour that
the *Tom Bowling*, with Plum at the
helm and Joe Westlake in full rig,
marching up and down the quarter-
deck, came leisurely rounding down
Halfway Reach before a pleasant
northerly breeze of wind blowing
over the flat, fat levels of Barking.
The *Tom Bowling*, opening Jenning-
tree Point, ported her helm and
floated in all her pride of white canvas and radiant metal and fathom
and a half of shining bunting at her
masthead into Erith Reach.

Just as she came abreast of Labour's Retreat a gun was fired ; the
white powder-smoke clouded the
tailor's lawn ; the thunder of the
ordnance smote the ear of Joe Westlake, who, dilating his nostrils and directing his eyes at Sloper's villa,
bawled out : " Peter ! that 's meant
for us, my heart ! Down hellum !
slacken away fore and aft ! pipe all
hands for action !"

A second gun roared upon the

lawn that sloped from the tailor's
house; and almost as loud was the
shout that Westlake delivered to all
hands to look alive and bring the
guns to bear. The *Tom Bowling*
was thrown into the wind and brought
to a stand abreast of Labour's Retreat; Plum took a turn with the
helm and went to help at the guns,
and in a few minutes the three of a
crew, with Westlake continuously
bawling out orders to bear a hand
and load again, were actively engaged in firing blank at the enemy on
the lawn.

It might have been that Mr. Sloper
and his friends were a little tipsy; it
might have been that they were irri-
tated by their *feu de joie* being interrupted and complicated, so to speak,
by the cutter's artillery; it is certain
that they continued to load and
discharge their guns as fast as they
could spunge them out; whilst from
the river the cutter maintained a
rapid fire at Labour's Retreat. In
an evil moment, temper getting the
better of Sloper's judgment, he loaded
one of his pieces with stones, and the
gun was so well aimed that on Joe
Westlake looking aloft he beheld his
beautiful flag of a fathom and a half
in holes.

For some moments the old man-of-warsman stood staring up at his wounded flag, idle with wrath and astonishment. He then in a voice of thunder shouted : " Plum—Robins —Tuck ! D' ye see what that there fired little tailor 's been and done ? Why, junk me if he ha' n't shot our colour through ! Boys, load with ball ; d' ye hear ? Suffocate me, but he shall have it back. Quick, my hearts, and go for him."

With ocean alacrity some round shot were got up, a gun was fired point-blank at Labour's Retreat, and down came a chimney-stack, amidst the cheers of the crew of the *Tom Bowling*.

"Now, then," roared old Joe, "over with our boat, lads, and board 'em ! Tommy, stay you here and let go the anchor " ; and in a very few minutes Plum and Robins were pulling Joe Westlake ashore.

Sloper and his party saw them coming and manfully stood their ground. The three seamen, securing their boat, forced their way on to the lawn and marched up to the tailor and his friends.

"What do you mean by firing at my cutter ?" roared old Joe.

"What do you mean by knocking down my chimneys ?" cried the tailor, who was exceedingly pale.

"Who began it?" bawled Joe.
"Who fired first? Who's bin and
made holes in that there flag of mine?
Why, that's the flag of a British
sailor, you little withered thimble
you; and durn ye, if you don't make
me instantly an humble apology and
stump up with the cost of what ye 've
injured, I 'll skin ye!" and he threw
himself into a very menacing posture.

At this point one of the tailor's
friends slunk off.

"My chimney-stack is worth more
than your twopenny flag," shrieked
Sloper, maddened even into some
temporary emotion of courage by
the insults of the old man-of-warsman.

"Say that again, will 'ee," said
Joe. "Just sneer at that there flag
again, will 'ee."

The tailor was idiotic enough to
repeat the affront, on which, and as
though a perfect understanding as to
what was to be done subsisted among
the three sailors, old Joe, Plum, and
Robins fell upon Sloper, and, lifting
him up in their arms, ran with him to
the boat, into which they flung him,
paying not the least heed whatever
to his cries for help and for mercy,
and instantly headed for the cutter,
leaving the tailor's friends white as

milk and speechless with alarm near the cannon upon the lawn.

When the boat reached the cutter, Plum jumped aboard and received little Sloper from the hands of old Joe, making no more of the burthen than had the tailor been a parcel, say, of a coat and waistcoat, or a pair of trousers. Old Joe then actively got over the rail. He lifted the little main-hatch, and Mr. Sloper was dropped into the space below, where the darkness was so great that he could not see, and where there was nothing to sit upon but Thames ballast.

"In boat, up anchor, and away with us!" said Joe Westlake.

The breeze was fresh, the cutter was always an excellent sailer, and in a very short space of time she was running down Long Reach with Erith and its adjacent shores out of sight, past the round of land where Dartford creek is to be found. Joe Westlake then called a council. Robins was at the tiller; Plum and Tuck came aft, and the four debated at the helm.

"I 've heerd," said old Joe, " of this tailor afore. His name 's Sloper. I 've never larnt why he mounted them guns, or where the little rooting hog got his pluck from to fire 'em.

But there can be no shadder of a doubt, mates, that his object in firing to-day was to insult that there flag."

He pointed with an immensely square forefinger to the masthead.

"Ne'er a shadder," said Plum.

"For why," continued old Joe, "did the smothered rag of a chap wait for us to come right abreast afore firing?"

"Ah! that's it, ye see," exclaimed Bob Robins. "There ye've hit it, Mr. Westlake."

"The little faggot's game," old Joe went on, "is as clear as mud in a wineglass. He fires with blank cartridge; like as he'd say ' What 'll *you* do?' What did he want? That we should retarn his civility with grape? Of course; that if it should come to a difficulty he'd have the law on his side. Not being able to aggravate us into shotting our guns, what must he turn to and do but load with stone—and look at that flag! Riddled, mates. I'll not speak of it as spiled, though a prettier and a better bit of bunting was never mastheaded. Spiled ain't the word : disgraced it is."

"Degraded," said Plum, in a deep voice.

"Ay, and degraded," cried old Joe, with a surly, dangerous nod.

2

"That there little tailor has degraded the honour of our flag. What 's to be done to him?"

After a pause, Plum said : " Bring him up and sit in examination on him. Try him fairly, and convict him."

They opened the hatch and pulled little Sloper off the Thames ballast into daylight. He was exceedingly white, and trembled violently, and cut, indeed, a very pitiful figure as he stood on the quarter-deck of the *Tom Bowling*, surveyed by her owner and crew. He was a short man and spare, and Tom Tuck grinned as he looked at him.

" I suppose you 're aweer," said old Joe, " that in shooting at my flag and wounding her you 've degraded the honour of it? Are you aweer of that?"

" You came in my way; I was shooting for my hentertainment," answered Mr. Sloper.

" You 're a retired tailor, ain't ye?" said Joe.

Sloper sulkily answered "Yes."

" Have ye any acquaintance with the laws which are made and pur-wided for British seamen when it happens that their flag 's degraded by the haction of a retired tailor?" said old Joe.

Mr. Sloper, instead of answering, cast a languishing eye at the river banks, which were fast sliding past, and requested to be set ashore.

"It don't answer his purpose to speak to the pint," said Plum.

" Listen, now," said old Joe, shaking his forefinger close into the face of little Sloper. "When a retired tailor degrades the honour of a seaman's flag by a shooting at it and a riddling of it, the law 'as made and purwided sets forth this : that the insulted sailor shall collect his crew and in the presence of all hands pass sentence after giving an impartial hearing to what the culprit may have to say in his defence. Now, you durned little powder-burner, speak up, and own what made you do it, and then I 'll pass judgment."

"What 's your game ? What d' yer mean to do with me ? Where are you carryin' me to ?" cried the owner of Labour's Retreat. "None of yer nonsense, you know. This is what 's called kidnappin'. It 's hindictable. You may find yourself in a very unpleasant predicament over this business, I can tell yer. You profess to know who I am. D' yer want to know what I 'm worth ? Yer 'd better put me ashore, I say, and stop this nonsense. I don't mind a joke, but this is carrying a lark too far. Why," he shrieked, "here we are a-drawing on to Northfleet! Yer 'd better let me go." And so he went on.

Old Joe and the others listened to him with stern faces ; in fact, they received his protests and threats as his defence. When he had made an end Joe Westlake spoke thus :

"Sloper—I dunno your Christian name and I won't demean myself by asking of it,—four of your country-men—and sorry they are that you should be a countrymen of their 'n — have patiently listened to what ye 've had to say. And all that ye 've said amounts to nothen at all. The hac-cusation made against ye is one of the very gravest as can be brought agin a retired tailor. You 're charged with degrading the honour of my flag, and ye 've been found guilty, and my sentence is that after a sufficient time 's been granted you for prayer and meditation, ye be brought up to the place of hexecution, aboard this here cutter the *Tom Bowling*, and hanged by the neck till you 're dead."

"Murder ! " screamed Sloper, and here (so he afterwards swore in court) the unhappy little tailor fell down upon his knees and begged Joe West-lake to grant him his life.

"Clap him under hatches," exclaimed the old man-of-warsman, and Plum and another, lifting the hatch cover, popped Mr. Sloper down among the ballast again.

By this time the afternoon had very considerably advanced, the wind had dropped, and it was already dark when the *Tom Bowling* let go her anchor off Gravesend. The cabin lamp was lighted, and old Joe and Plum sat down to a hearty meal, after which they smoked their pipes and dipped a ladle into a silver bowl of rum punch of Westlake's own brewing.

"D' ye mean, captain," said Plum, "that the little chap in the hold shall have any supper?"

"Well, Peter," answered old Joe, "I 've bin a-turning of it over in my mind, and spite of his 'rageous conduct I dunno, after all, that it would be right to let him lie all night without a bite of something. Call Bob."

This man, whose surname was Robins, arrived. Joe told him to get a lantern and cut a plate of beef and bread and mix a small mug of rum and water.

"Ye can tell the little chap, Bob," said old Joe, speaking with one eye shut, "that we 're only a-feeding of him up so as to get more satisfaction out of his hexecution to-morrow morning. You can say that sailoring is a rather monotonous life, and that if he 'll die game we shall all feel obliged for the hentertainment he 'll afford us."

Whether Bob Robins communicated this speech to Sloper I cannot say. It is certain, however, that he took the lantern and the tailor's supper into the hold and stood over the little man whilst he ate and drank. When the retired tailor had finished his repast he asked Robins if he was to be kept locked up in that black hole all night without anything to lie on but shingle.

" What did you fire at us for ? " said Bob.

" I never fired at you. I was firing for my own diversion," answered Mr. Sloper.

" D' ye load with stones for your divarsion, as ye call it ? " said Bob.

" There was no stones when you came along," cried the tailor. " Why did you aggrevate me by firing in return ? "

" What did you want to fire at all for ? " said Bob, almost pitying the trembling little creature as he showed by the lantern light in the cutter's small black hold.

" I was celebrating a hanniversary," answered Mr. Sloper, who mal-

treated his *h's* as badly as old Westlake.

"And what sort of a hanniversary
calls for gun firing ?" said Bob, holding up the lantern to the tailor's face.

"It was the hanniversary of my
wife's death," said Mr. Sloper, "and
a day of rejoicing with me and my
friends."

Bob, who himself was a married
man, loving his wife and two little
girls with the warm affection of the
genuine sailor's heart, looked for some
moments speechless with disgust at
the white shadowy countenance of
Mr. Sloper, and without deigning another word, rose through the hatch,
which he carefully secured, and then
went aft to old Joe and Plum to report what had passed.

"Smite me," cried the old man-of-
warsman, after listening to Bob ;
"but if this was furrin parts instead
of Lunnon river, poisoned if I
would n't yard arm the little faggot in
rale earnest. What ! make a joyful
hanniversary of his wife's death, and
fire off guns that the whole blooming
country may know what a little beast
it is. Sit ye down, Bob, there's a
glass—help yourself. This is what
we mean to do," and he forthwith
related his scheme for the morning
to Robins and Plum.

They smoked hard and roared out in great peals of laughter. The bulkheads of a little ship such as the *Tom Bowling* are not, as may be supposed, of very formidable scantling; there is no doubt that Sloper in the hold heard these wild shouts of laughter which the muffling of the bulkhead and his own terrors would render awful to him, and we may be sure that as he lay in the blackness harkening to those horrid notes of merriment, he feared and perspired exceedingly.

Somewhere at about eight o'clock next morning the *Tom Bowling* was got under way, and when all hands had breakfasted, Joe Westlake took the tiller, and Plum, Robins, and Tuck went to work to construct the machinery for the retired tailor's execution. They filled a big tub with water and covered it loosely with a tarpaulin. Close against this tub they placed a three-legged stool; alongside this stool upon the deck was a tar-bucket with a tar-brush sticking up in it; they also procured and placed beside this tar-bucket a piece of rough iron hoop. At the time that these preparations were completed the cutter was running through the Warp, which is some little distance past the Nore Light.

The river had widened into the
aspect of an ocean, and over the
bows of the craft the water stretched
boundless and blue as the horizon of
the Pacific.

They opened the hatch and brought
the tailor on deck. Needless to say,
he had not slept a wink all night.
Who, accustomed to a feather-bed,
could snatch even ten minutes' sleep
when his couch is Thames ballast?
Sloper's eyes were bloodshot, and his
countenance haggard. He looked in-
conceivably grimy and forlorn, and
Bob Robins felt sorry for the little
creature till he recollected on a sudden the man's reason for letting off
his cannons. Tuck took the helm,
and old Joe with a solemn countenance and slow gait rolled forward to
where the apparatus was stationed.

" Now, you see your fate," he exclaimed, lifting up his eyes as though
he beheld a rope with a noose
dangling from the masthead, " and
since no good can come of caution-
ing a corpse, why then, sorry I am
that there are n't a company of people arter your kind assembled aboard
this craft to witness the hexecution of
my sentence upon ye. Last night I
heard that the reason of your firing
off your guns were to celebrate the
hanniversary of your wife's death. I

dunno, I'm sure, whether such a practice would n't be considered as more criminal and worthy of a fearfuller punishment than even the shooting at a man's flag and degrading the honour of it. But to say more 'ud only be a-wasting of breath. My lads, do your duty."

Robins, with powerful arms, grasped the tailor, who shrieked murder and struggled hard. His struggles were as the throes and convulsions of a mouse in the teeth of a cat. He was dumped down on the three-legged stool. In an instant Plum lathered his jaws with the tar-brush, and picking up the piece of broken iron hoop scraped little Sloper's cheeks till the lather was as much blood as tar. Then, lifting his leg, he tilted the stool and Mr. Sloper fell backwards on to the tarpaulin, which, yielding to his weight, soused him into the water. They left him to kick and splash awhile, then pulled him out and ran him forward into the head, where they secured him to the windlass till the sun should have somewhat dried him.

But long before the sun had had time to comfort the shivering little creature Herne Bay had hove into sight. The helm was shifted, and the cutter ran close into the land, where

they hove her to whilst Plum and
Robins got the boat over.

Mr. Sloper was then dropped over
the side into the boat, which pulled
ashore, landed him, and returned ;
and a few minutes later the cutter
was standing for the mouth of the
river, leaving the tailor on the Herne
Bay beach, forty miles from home
without a farthing in his pocket.

This is the historic incident of the
Thames which I desire to rescue from
the oblivion that has overtaken many
greater matters.   Mr. Sloper, on his
return to Labour's Retreat, and when
he was somewhat recovered in nerves
and health, sued Joe Westlake in the
Whitechapel County Court, in action
of tort, laying his damages at the
moderate sum of fifty pounds.   Mr.
G. E. Williams, for the defendant,
contended that the plaintiff deserved
the treatment which he had brought
on himself, and the Judge, after hearing the evidence, said that although
the plaintiff, Sloper, had acted most
improperly in loading his guns, the
defendant, Westlake, had retaliated
too severely, but, under the circumstances, he should award only five
pounds' damages, without costs.

Cornered!

"I DON'T see no signs of the tug, do you, Tom?" said the old skipper, John Bunk, rolling up to me from the companion hatchway. He was fresh from the cabin, and was rather tipsy, with a fixed stare and a stately manner, though his legs would have framed the lower part of an egg. His hat was tall, and brushed the wrong way. He wore a thick shawl round his neck and was wrapped up in a long monkey-jacket, albeit we were in the dog-days. In a word, Bunk was a skipper of a type that is fast perishing off our home waters.

"No," said I, "there's no sign of the tug."

"Then bloomed," said he, "if I don't work her up myself. Who's afraid? I know the ropes. Get amidships in the fair-way and keep all on, and there y' are. And mubbe the tug 'll pick us up as we go."

"It's all one to Tom," said I.

Our brig was the *Venus*, of Rye, a stump topgallantmast coaster, eighty years old. We were in a big bight of the coast, heading for a river which flows past a well known town, whither we were bound. The bed of that river went in a vein through about three miles of mud, till it sheared into the land, and flowed into a proper-looking river with banks of its own. At flood the water covered the mud, but the river was buoyed, and when once you had the land on either hand and the bay of mud astern, the pilot-age to the town was no more than a matter of bracing the yards about till you floated into one long reach whose extremity was painted by the red wharf you moored alongside of.

We were six of a ship's company. John Bunk was skipper, I, Tom Fish, was the mate, the others were Bill Martin, Jack Stevens, a man named Rooney, and a boy called William. On board craft of this sort there is very little discipline, and the sailors talk to the captain as though he lived in the forecastle.

"John," sings out Bill Martin, casting his eyes over the greasy yellow surface of the water streaming shorewards, "are ye going to try for it without the tug?"

"Ay," answered old Bunk.

"And quite right, tew. No good a-messing about here all day," says Jack Stevens at the tiller.

The land was flat and treeless on either hand the river, but it rose, about a couple of miles off, curving into a front of glaring chalk, with a small well known town sparkling in the distance like a handful of frost in a white split. The horizon astern was broken by the moving bodies of many ships in full sail, and the sky low down was hung with the smoke of vanished steamers as though the stuff was cobwebs black with dust.

The stream was the turn of the flood. Old Bunk went forward into the bows, and the brig flapped forwards creaking like a basket on the small roll of the shallow water. We overhung her rails, and watched for ourselves. John Bunk, trying to look dignified with the drink in him, stared stately ahead; sometimes singing out to the helmsman to port, and then to starboard, and so we washed on, fairly hitting the river's mouth, and stemming safely for a mile, till the flat coast was within an easy scull of our jolly-boat, and you saw the spire of a church, and a few red roofs amidst a huddle of trees on the right, at that time two miles distant.

Just then the *Venus* took the mud; she grounded just as a huge fat sow knuckles quietly ere stretching herself.

"All aback forrard!" sings out Bill Martin, with a loud silly laugh.

We were a brig of a hundred and eighty tons, and there was nothing to be done with poling; nor was kedging going to help us at this the first quarter of ebb.

"Tom," says John Bunk, coming aft and speaking cheerfully, "there's no call to make any worrit over this shining job. The tug's bound to be coming along afore sundown, anyhow. See that village there?" says he, pointing. "My brother lives in that village, at a public house of his own, called the 'Eight Bells,' and seeing as we're hard and fast, I shall take the boys on a visit to him and leave you and William to look arter the brig."

"Suppose the tug should come along?" said I.

"She could do nothing with us till the flood floats us," said he; "I shall let go the anchor for security and go ashore."

He talked like a reckless old fool, but was tipsy, and in no temper to reason with. The situation of the brig was safe enough as far as ocean and weather went; nothing could hurt her as she lay mud-cradled on her fat bilge. We clewed up and let the canvas hang by its rigging, and then dropped the anchor; after which old Bunk and the others cleaned themselves up and got the boat over, and went away in her, singing songs, leaving me and William to look after the brig.

It was ten o'clock in the morning, a very fine hot day. I went into the cabin for a smoke, and after lounging an hour or so below whilst the boy boiled a piece of beef for our dinner, I stepped on deck, and found that the sea was already half-way out of the bay with twenty lines of foaming ripples purring not a quarter of a mile off, and the channel of the river was already plain, coming out from the land, and through the dry mud like a lane of water till it met the wash of the yellow brine and melted into it. The brig lay with an uncomfortable list to starboard. When the mud should come a-dry it would be an easy jump from her decks to it.

At half-past twelve William came below with my dinner, and I told the lad to out with his knife and eat with me. We munched together, taking it easy. There was nothing to be done on deck, no sign of the tug, no use we could put her to, even if she should heave into sight, and the time hung heavy. After dinner I lay upon a locker smoking, and William sat at the table with a pipe in his mouth.

Presently I thought I heard a noise
of something moving in a scratching
sort of way on deck. I listened and
then heard nothing. A little later,
happening to be looking at William,
I heard the same noise, and that
moment I fancied a kind of shadow
passed over the glass of the grimy
little cabin skylight.

I said to William : " Step on deck,
my lad, and see if anybody 's come
aboard."

He went up, and was not gone a
minute when I heard him scream
shockingly. The shriek was full of
terror and agony, and froze my blood.
I rushed on deck and saw the figure
of William under the paw of a large
yellow tiger ! I stared madly, as
though my senses were all gone
wrong and reporting a nightmare.
But the big beast, turning its head,
spied me, swept the planks with its
tail, crouched in cat-like way, and
was coming for me.

With a roar of terror I sprang for
the main rigging, and in a few breathless moments was safe in the top.

It was all sheer mud now to the
very forefoot of the brig ; but the
half of her lay afloat in the stream of
the river. I saw the marks of the
beast's paws pitting the shiny surface
of ooze and sand ; the trail came in

3

a straight line from the land to the right of the village where Bunk's brother lived to the starboard bow of the brig. The beast had sprung easily aboard. We were not in India, nor in Africa, nor in any country where such huge yellow horrors as that flourished ; therefore, on recovering my wits and my breath whilst I looked down over the rim of the top, I guessed that the tiger had broken loose from some show or menagerie, and had made for this desolate waste of sand to escape the hunt that was doubtless in loud cry after him. But I could not get any comfort into me out of the reflection that we had stranded on English instead of African or South American mud ; down on deck, now crouching close beside the boy without, however, offering to touch the motionless figure, was a massive savage beast, apparently a man-eater ; and it was all the same to me whether it had sprung aboard off the banks of an Indian river, or trotted across this breast of English slime out of a showman's cage.

The boy lay as though dead, and I turned sick, fearing to see the creature eat him. I was going to call, thinking he would answer me, then reflected if he was not dead my voice

might cause him to move, and bring
the tiger upon him, and so I lay
silent in the top, now staring down,
then glaring round upon the scene of
mud and at the distant blue crescent
of sea for the help that was nowhere
visible.

Presently the tiger got up, and,
passing over the body of the lad,
stepped with its supple gait into the
bows. I took my chance of shouting
to William, but the lad never stirred.
Again and again I yelled down at
him, and I saw the splendid, horrible
beast in the bows gazing at me, and
still the lad remained lifeless. He
was upon his face, with his arms out,
as though his hands were nailed to
the deck. I looked for blood, but
saw none.

The most awful time that ever
passed in my life now went along.
The tiger roamed the deck silently,
smelling at everything, once shoving
its huge head into the companion-
way, and I prayed with all my heart
it would go below, that I might skim
to the hatch and secure it. It drew
its head out, and going to the boy
stopped and smelt him. The very
blood in me was curdled, for I made
sure the beast was about to eat the
lad. Sometimes I broke out into the
noisiest roarings and screaming my

pipes could set up in the hope of driving the brute overboard.

Between five and six o'clock in the evening the tide had made so as to cover the mud, and I saw the brig's boat approaching. Those who pulled flourished their oars drunkenly. The boat came to a stand when within easy hailing distance, as though old Bunk was taking a view of me as I sat in the top, and was wondering what I did there.

I roared out : "For God's sake mind how you come aboard ! There's been a blooming tiger in this brig since noon ! "

" A what ? " yelled Bunk, and the seamen pulled a little closer in.

It was still broad flaming daylight, and the sun hung like a huge blood-red target over the crimson sea.

" A what ? " shrieked Bunk.

" A tiger ! A blooming tiger ! " I bellowed, pointing to the brute that lay crouched on the forecastle hidden from the boat's crew.

" Drunk again, Tom ? or is it sun-stroke this time ? " sung out old Bunk, standing up in the boat and lurching to the rocking of her.

" It 's killed William ! " I yelled.

When I said this the beast, attracted by the noise of voices over the side,

got up and looked over the bulwark
rail at the men, and old Bunk
instantly saw it. He stared for a
minute or two as though he had been
blasted by a stroke of lightning.
The other three fellows then saw the
beast, and if there was any drink in
their heads the fumes of it flew out at
that sight, and left them sober men.
Their postures were full of wild surprise and terror whilst they gazed.
Old Bunk roared :

"Has he killed the boy, d' yer
say ?"

"He lies there dead," cried I,
pointing. "He has n't moved since
I first saw him."

"Has he been eating of him ?"

"No!"

"We must go ashore for help,"
sung out Jack Stevens.

"For God's sake don't leave me up
here!" I cried.

"Tom," shouted Bunk, "there 's
only wan thing to dew ; there 's an
old gun in my cabin, and yer 'll find
a powder-flask and ball in the locker.
We must keep that tiger a-watching
of us over the bow, whilst you run
below and shut the hatch. By lifting
the lid you 'll be able to shoot him
through the skylight. Come you
down now as far as you durst whilst

we fixes the attention of the brute upon ourselves."

I at once dropped into the rigging, where I stretched and played my legs a bit. They were as stiff as hand-spikes after that long spell in the maintop. I descended as low down as the sheer-pole, breathlessly watch-ing. They pulled the boat under the bow, and Bill Martin with lifted oar made as though spearing at the brute's head. It opened its huge mouth and showed its immense claws upon the rail ; old Bunk hissed and snapped at it, then roared out to me :

" Now 's your time, Tom," whilst I heard Jack Stevens sing out :

" Back astarn ! The fired cat 's going to jump."

With the nimbleness of terror I dropped to the deck and passed like a shadow to the hatch, unnoticed by the beast. In a moment I closed the companion doors, then entering Bunk's cabin found the gun and ammunition. I loaded the piece, and, getting on to the cabin table, put my head into the skylight, and bawled out to let the others know that I was going to shoot. My voice attracted the tiger ; it turned, and with sway-ing tail came with velvet tread, crouching in a springing posture. I levelled the gun, steadying the barrel, and, taking a cool, deliberate aim—for I was safe!—fired, and the instant I had fired, without pausing to see what had happened, I loaded again ; but before I could present the piece for a second shot the beast, who was now on this side the boy, lurched and fell.

I fired a second ball into it, and then a third and a fourth, and now shouting to let the men know the brute was wounded and dying, I ran on deck, and putting the muzzle of the gun to the creature's glazing eye, fired, and this did its business, for just one spasm ran through it, and then the terrible, muscular bulk lay motionless.

The men came scrambling aboard. We turned the boy over, and took him below. Shortly afterwards the tug hove in sight, and we let the beast lie whilst we got our anchor and manœuvred with the tow-rope. I am sorry to say the boy was dead. On our arrival a doctor came and looked at him, and a crowd tumbled aboard to view the beast. There was not a scratch on the lad ; the tiger had never touched him ; the doctor said he had died of syncope caused by fright.

The owner of the tiger threatened old Bunk with the law, and asked for a hundred guineas. Bunk started William's mother upon him for compensation for the loss of her boy, and shortly afterwards the showman went broke.

A Midnight Visitor.

"THERE are more terrors at sea than shipwreck and fire, more frights and horrors, mateys, than famine, blindness, and cholera," said the old seaman with a slow motion of his eyes round upon the little company of sailors. "I remember a line of poetry—'a thing of beauty is a joy for ever.' Can any man here tell me who wrote that? Well, I suppose it is a joy so long as it remains a beauty, but d'ye see it's got to remain, and that's the job.

"Yet, mates, if there is a thing of beauty that should be a joy to every heart, it is a full-rigged ship, clothed in white, asleep in the light of the moon, on a pale and silent breast of ocean that waves in splendour under the planet over the flying jibboom end. Have I got such a ship as that in my mind? Ay. And was it a sheet calm but ne'er a moon? Ay, again. There was ne'er a moon that night. The ship rose faint and hushed to the stars. It was one bell in the morning watch. Scarce air enough moved to give life to the top-most canvas ; as the ship bowed upon the light swell the sails swung in and swung out with a rushing sound of many wings up in the gloom. Yet the vessel had steerage way in that hour. Shall I tell you why ? Because I know !

"And ere that full-rigged ship alone in the middle of the Indian Ocean came to a dead halt, life sinking in her with the failing of the wind in a sort of dying shudder from royal to course, this was how her decks showed : a man was at the wheel, the chief mate leaned against the rail in the thickness made by the mizzen rigging, and with folded arms seemed to doze in the shadow ; a 'young gentleman,' as they used to call the 'brass-bounders,' loafed sleepily near the main shrouds where the break of the poop came. That youngster watched the stars trembling between the squares of the starboard rigging. He was new to the sea, and emotion and sentiment were still sweet—they were not salt in him. He was the son of a gentleman—he had a clever eye for what was picturesque and romantic, for what was tender and affecting in all he beheld, whether by

day or night, whether he looked aloft
or whether upon the mighty breast of
brine—he should have done well : he
oughter ha' done well."

The grey-haired respectable seaman closed his eyes in a silence filled
with significance, and after a short
smoke thus proceeded :

"Some of the watch on deck
sprawled about in the shadow out of
sight, curled up, asleep ; only one
figure was upright forward. 'T was
the shape of the man on the look-out.
For all the world he postured like the
mate aft, as though he copied the
officer for a life or death bet : head
sunk, arms folded—the forecastle
break brought that raised deck well
aft, and the look-out had the shadow
of the starboard fore-rigging upon
him.

"This man thus standing, by no
means asleep, yet with his head sunk
and no doubt his eyes closed, was
suddenly struck on the side of the
face by something hairy, damp, and
cold. He sprang into the air as
though he had been shot through the
heart. O heavens ! What was it ?
A naked figure, shaggy as Peter Sar-
rano, wild with hair, furious with a
grin, terrible with the red gleams
the starlight flung upon his little eyes.
The sailor shrieked like a midnight

cat and fell in a heap down upon the deck in a fit.

"The ship was in commotion in an instant. Such a yell as that was worse than the smell of fire.

" ' What 's the matter? ' bawled the mate from the break of the poop.

"A number of shadowy shapes swarmed up the forecastle ladder. Meanwhile the watch below, aroused by the yell of the look-out man, suspecting imminent deadly danger in the peculiar noise, were leaping in twos and threes up through the fore-scuttle, growling and swearing and grumbling, and asking of one another in those deep hurricane-chested whispers which will make a stagnant midnight atmosphere tingle, what the blooming blazes that noise was, and what was up.

" ' What 's the matter? ' roared the mate.

" ' Here 's Kennedy in a fit, sir,' sung out a voice.

" ' Is that all ? ' said the mate, and he went forward to look at the man.

" ' It 's a fit certainly,' said he. ' Give him air, lads. Get a drink of cold water into his mouth. It 's epilepsy.'

" ' Or weevils,' said a deep voice.

"The joker was not to be discerned ; the mate therefore took no notice. Some one brought a pannikin of cold water, and after a little the man came to, by which time the watch below had returned to their hammocks, and the forecastle was comparatively clear.

" When the mate was told the man had his senses and was sitting up, he went forward again and questioned him. He was sitting on the foot of a cathead, and was too weak to rise when the mate stood before him.

" ' What is this you 're rambling about?' said the officer. 'Are n't you quite well yet?'

" 'S' 'elp me then, it slapped me fair over the chops, like flicking yer with the wet sleeve of a jacket. He rose four foot when I swounded. He might ha' been more an' he might ha' been less. Darkness put him out, only that I recollect,' said the man, turning up his pale face to the stars, 'taking notice of a couple of eyes like red lights floating in water and a grin of teeth wide as the keys of a pianey.'

" 'He 's mad,' thought the mate, who stepped nevertheless into the bows and looked over. Nothing was to be seen. He surveyed the ocean by the light of the stars, and glanced along the deck and up aloft, then told the look-out man to go below and turn in, and went aft, reckoning the thing an epileptic's nightmare.

" 'It soaks into their livers ashore,' thought he, as he leisurely mounted the poop ladder, 'and when they get upon the ocean and into hot weather it works out in slaps over the head and hairy sea-beasts four feet high. Ha! ha! ha!' and he laughed drowsily as he walked to the wheel.

" Just then a catspaw blew. It was so faint that it scarcely chilled the moistened forefinger of the officer. It had to be reckoned with nevertheless; it was an air of wind anyhow, and some one sung out that the ship was aback forward, on which the mate went to the break of the poop, and yelled to the seamen to trim sail. Something went wrong in swinging the yards on the fore.

" 'Jump aloft, a hand, and clear it.'

" A seaman went up the rigging, his shadowy shape vanished in the gloom that blackened like a thunder-cloud upon the foretop ; he showed again when he got into the topmast rigging, with his figure small, and clear-cut against the stars.

"Suddenly, when midway the rigging he yelled at the top of his voice. His cry was more dismal and heart-shaking than even that with which the

man Kennedy had terrified the ship ;
he caught hold of a backstay, and
sank to the bulwark rail, as though
handsomely lowered away in a bowline.

"'By Cott!' he roared, flinging
down his cap, whilst those who
peered close saw that he trembled
violently, ' der toyfel is on boardt dis
ship. I have seen her mit mine eyes.
If I hov not seen her den I was a
nightmare und she was mad. Look
up dar.'

"He obtained no answer. The
seamen attending the indication of
the Dutchman were to a man gazing
aloft with hanging chins ; for on high
up in the cross-trees, a visible bulk
of shadow, there sat, squatted, hung
—what? A man? No angel from
heaven surely? A demon then with
folded wings like those of a bat resting in his flight from the halls of fire
to some star of Satan? Mateys, if
you think this language too poetical,
I 'll translate my thought into fok'sle
speech. But I 'd rather leave the job
to others," said the grey-haired respectable seaman ; "I 've forgotten
the profanities of the sea-parlour. I
have not used a bad word for thirty
year."

Some interruption by laughter attended this flight. The grey-haired

sailor looked round him with his slow critical motion of eye, and continued :

"'What 's wrong aloft forrad there?' bawled the mate, and now he sung out with energy and decision, for the figure of the captain was alongside of him.

"'There 's something aloft that looks like a man,' howled a seaman, one of the upstaring crowd about the Dutchman. 'Come forrad, sir. You 'll see him.'

"The mate and the captain went forward and looked up.

"'It 's a man,' exclaimed the captain. 'Aloft there ! What are you doing skylarking up in those crosstrees? Come down !' he cried, angrily.

"'You sick-hearts, what d'ye see to stare at, or seeing, why don't you go for it?' thundered the mate, after a pause, during which the figure on high had made no answer or motion, and as he spoke the words the officer bounded on to the bulwarks, and ran up the fore-shrouds.

"He travelled with heroic speed till he got as high as the foretop. There he stood at gaze ; presently, after you might have counted fifty, putting his foot into the topmast rigging he began to crawl, with frequent breathless stops; his passage up those shrouds had the dying uncertainty of the tread of a blue-bottle when it climbs a sheet of glass in October.

"On a sudden he came down into the top very fast. There he stood staring aloft as though fascinated or electrified, then putting his foot over the top he got into the fore-shrouds, and trotted down on deck, all very quick. The captain stood near the main hatch, looking up. The mate approached him, and, in a whisper of awe and terror, exclaimed, whilst his eyes sought the shadow up in the foretopmast cross-trees, 'I believe the Dutchman's right, sir, and that we've been boarded by the devil himself.'

"'What are you talking about?'

"'I never saw the like of such a thing,' said the mate, in shaking tones.

"'Is it a man?' said the captain, staring up with amazement, while the seamen came hustling close in a sneaking way to listen, and the Dutchman drew close to the mate.

"'It has the looks of a man,' said the mate; 'yet it sha'n't be murder if you kill him.'

"'She vos no man, sir. I vos close. I vent closer don you. I oxpect, sir,' said the Dutchman, 'she 's an imp. Strange dot I did not see him till I was upon her.'

" The captain went swiftly to his cabin for a binocular glass. The lenses helped him to determine the motionless shadow in the cross-trees, and he clearly distinguished an apparently large human shape, but in what fashion, or whether or not habited, it was impossible to see. How had he come into the ship? The captain went on to the poop and searched the silent sea with the glass with some fancy of finding a boat within reach of his vision. Nothing was to be seen but the glass-smooth face of the deep, with here and there the light of a large trembling star draining into it. The catspaw had died out, and it mattered nothing whether they braced the fore-yards round or not.

" It got wind in the forecastle that something wild, unearthly, hellish, was aloft, and the watch below turned out, too restless to sleep, and all through those hours of darkness the sailors walked the decks in groups, again and again staring up at the foretopmast cross-trees, where the mysterious bulk of blackness sate, squatted, or hung motionless, like some brooding fiend, or incarnation of ill-luck, sinking by force of meditation its curses not loud, but deep, into the bottom of the very hold itself.

"'Why don't the captain let me shoot him?' said the second mate at four o'clock. 'I cannot miss that mark; my rifle will bring him to your feet at the cost of a single shot.'

"'No,' said the chief mate, 'I 've talked of trying what shooting will do. The captain means to wait for sunlight. But how did it get on board?' said he, sinking his voice in awe. 'There 's no land for hundreds of leagues. Is it some sort of human sea-monster, some merman whose looks blind you with their ugliness, which this ship 's been doomed to discover, and perhaps carry home?'

"It was not long before day whitened the east. In those climates the morning is a quick revelation, and hardly had the dawn broke when sea and sky were lighted up. And then, and even then, what was it? There it sat up in the cross-trees, a hairy, sulky bulk of man or beast, black, and the creature looked hard down whilst all hands were staring hard up.

"'Seized if it is n't a gorilla!' said the mate.

" 'No.' said the captain, letting
fall his binocular, 'look for yourself. Yet, it 's not a man, either.'
He burst into a laugh as though for
relief. 'It 's a huge, hairy baboon,
one of the biggest I ever saw in my
life. He 'll be as fierce as a muti-
nous crew, and strong as a frigate's
complement. What 's to be done
with him ? '

" 'How in Egypt did he come on
board ? ' said the mate, viewing the
beast through the glass.

" ' By that, maybe, sir,' exclaimed
the second mate, pointing to some
object floating flat and yellow, faint
and far out upon the starboard quarter.

" The captain levelled the ship's
telescope. ' A large raft ! ' he exclaimed, after some minutes of silent
examination. ' Take a boat and examine it '

" A quarter-boat was lowered, and
the second mate and four men pulled
away for the raft in the distance. It
was a very large raft, manifestly
launched by some country wallah in
the last throes : a complicate huge
grating, or floating platform, of immensely thick bamboos and spare
spars, secured by turns of Manilla or
coir rope. It was clean swept ; not a

rag was to be seen. Whether the
sufferers had been taken off, leaving
the baboon behind them, whether
they had died, and the wash of the
ocean had slipped their bodies overboard, the baboon holding on to the
raft, who was to tell? 'At sea,' said
Lord Nelson, 'nothing is impossible
and nothing improbable.'

"The raft had floated to the bows
of the ship in the silent midnight,
and the baboon sprang aboard and
aloft.

"The creature on high was a clear
picture in the bright sunshine. It
made many dreadful grimaces, by
the exhibition of its teeth, and when
the boat drew alongside it moved and
stood up, and showed a great tail,
then hung with one fist, looking down.
It next descended with the velocity of
wind into the foretop.

"The captain said: 'The beast
don't seem faint, but I guess he's
thirsty, and he may fall mad, come
down, and bite some of us. So,' says
he to the chief officer, 'send a hand
aloft with a bucket of fresh water for
the poor brute and a pocketful of
ship's bread. If we can civilise him,
so much the better.'

"But it never came to it," said
the grey-haired respectable seaman,

" The creature fled to the cross-trees nimble as light when he saw a couple of seamen mounting to the top, then descended, and ate and drank ravenously when they had come down, which feeding murdered him, and ruined the captain's hopes of carrying the fellow to London and selling him at a large price to the Zoölogical Gardens. For he refused to come on deck. He bared his teeth, and his eyes shone with the malice of hell if the men attempted to approach him. It was impossible to let him rest aloft throughout the night to command the ship, so to speak ; for he might sink to the deck stealthy as the shadow of a cloud blown by the wind, and he was strong enough and big enough to tear a sleeping man's throat out.

" ' He must be shot,' said the captain, and he told the second mate to fetch his rifle.

" The second mate, that he might make sure of his aim, went aloft into the foretop. The beast was then sitting on the topgallant yard. He had been in command of the fabric of the fore all day. Had it come on to blow so as to oblige the captain to shorten sail, the deuce a seaman durst have gone aloft to stow the canvas. The second mate, standing in the top, was

in the act of lifting his rifle, when the
monster, running on all fours out to
the dizzy topgallant yard-arm, stood
erect a breathless instant, poised—in
human posture—a marvellous picture
of the man-beast against the liquid
blue, then sprang into the air.

"'Come down,' roared the captain
to the second mate, 'and shoot him
through the head, for God's sake!'

"As the beast rose with a wild grin
after having been so long out of sight
through the frightful height he had
jumped from, you 'd have thought
he 'd have risen with a burst skin,
the captain bawled out, 'Blessed if
he 's not making for his raft.'

"The baboon, with a fixed expression, and with eyes askew upon the
ship as he drove past, swimming
very finely with long easy flourishes
of his arms and dexterous thrusts of
his legs, whilst the end of his tail
stood up astern of him as though it
was some comical little man there
steering,—the baboon, I say, was undoubtedly and with amazing sagacity
making straight for the raft, having
taken its bearings when aloft; but at
the moment the second mate knelt
to level his piece, meaning to murder
the poor brute out of pure mercy, the
thing uttered, oh, my God! what a

horrible cry ! and vanished, and a
quantity of blood rose and dyed a
bright patch upon the calm blue. No
more was seen of the baboon, but a
little later the black scythe-like fins
of three sharks showed in the spot
where he had disappeared."

Plums from a Sailor's Duff.

IT has been commonly expected of
sailors in all ages that they should
encounter nothing upon the
ocean but hair-breadth escapes. The
theory is that the mariner but half
discharges his duties when his experiences are limited to his work as
a seaman. That he may be fully and
perfectly accomplished vocationally
he must know what it is to have been
cast away, to have barely come off with
his life out of a ship on fire, to have
been overboard on many occasions in
heavy seas, to have chewed pieces of
lead in open boats to assuage his
thirst—to have encountered, in short,
most of the stock horrors of the
oceanic calling. Considering, however, that the sailor goes to sea holding his life in his hands, I cannot
but think that his mere occupation is
perilous enough to satisfy the romantic demands of the shoregoing
dreamer. It is feigned that the sea-

faring life is not one jot more dangerous than most of the laborious
callings followed ashore. Let no man
credit this. The sailor never springs
aloft, never slides out to a yard-arm,
never gives battle to the thunderous
canvas, scarcely performs a duty, indeed, that does not contain a distinct
menace to his life. That the calling
has less of danger in it in these days
than it formerly held I will not un-
dertake to determine. If in former
times ships put to sea destitute of the
scientific equipment which character-
ises the fabrics of this age, the mariner supplied the deficiencies of the
shipyard by caution and patience.
He was never in a hurry. He waited
with a resigned countenance upon
the will of the wind. He plied his
lead and log-line with indefatigable
diligence. There was no prompt de-
spatch in his day, no headlong thundering, through weather as thick as
mud in a wineglass, to reach his port.
We have diminished many of the
risks he ran through imperfect appli-
ances, but, on the other hand, we
have raised a plentiful stock of our
own, so that the balance between
then and now shows pretty level.

My seafaring experiences covered
about eight years, and they hit a tra-
ditional period of immense moment

—I mean the gradual transformation of the marine fabric from wood into iron. I was always afloat in wood, however, and never knew what it was to have an iron plate between me and the yearning wash of the brine outside until I went on a voyage to Natal and back in a big ocean steamer that all day long throbbed to the maddened heart in her engine room, like some black and gleaming leviathan rendered hysterical by the lances of whalers feeling for its life, and all night stormed through the dark ocean shadow like a body of fire, faster than a gale of wind could in my time have driven the swiftest clipper keel that furrowed blue water.

What hair-breadth escapes did I meet with? I have been asked. Was I ever marooned? Ever cast away, as Jack says, on the top crust of a half-penny loaf? Ever overboard among sharks? Ever gazing madly round the horizon, the sole occupant of a frizzling boat, in search of a ship where I might obtain water to cool my blue and frothing lips? Well, my duff is not a very considerable one, and the few plums in it I fear are almost wide enough apart to be out of hail of one another. However a sample or two will suffice to enable

me to keep my word and to write
something at all events autobio-
graphic.

So let us start off Cape Horn on a
July day in the year of grace 1859.
The ship was a fine old Australian
liner, a vessel of hard upon 1400
tons, a burden that in those days con-
stituted a large craft. She was commanded by one Captain Neatby,
something of a favourite I believe in
the passenger trade—a careful old
man with bow-legs and a fiery grog-
blossom of a nose. He wore a tall
chimney-pot hat in all weathers, and
was reckoned a very careful man because he always furled his fore and
mizzen royals in the first dog-watch
every night. We were a long way
south ; I cannot remember the exact
latitude, but I know it was drawing
close upon sixty degrees. There was
a talk in the midshipmen's berth
amongst us that the captain was trying
his hand at the great Circle course,
but none of us knew much about it
down in that gloomy, 'tween-decks,
slush-flavoured cavern in which we
youngsters lived. I was fourteen years
old, homeward bound on my first
voyage ; a little bit of a midshipman,
burnt dry by Pacific suns, with a
mortal hatred and terror of the wild,
inexpressibly bitter cold of the roar-

ing ice-loaded parallels in whose
Antarctic twilight our noble ship was
plunging and rolling now under a
fragment of maintopsail, now under
a reefed foresail and double-reefed
foretopsail, chased by the shrieking
western gale that flew like volleys of
scissors and thumbscrews over our
taffrail, and by seas, whose glittering,
flickering peaks one looked up at
from the neighbourhood of the wheel
as at the brows of tall and beetling
cliffs. The gale was white with snow,
and dark with the blinding fall of it
too, when I came on deck at noon.
I was in the chief mate's, or port
watch, as it is called. The ship was
running under a double-reefed topsail
—in those days we carried single sails,
—reefed foresail, close-reefed foretopsail, and maintopmast staysail.
The snow made a London fog of the
atmosphere ; forward of the galley
the ship was out of sight at times
when it came thundering down out of
the blackness aft, white as any smother
of spume. She pitched with the
majesty of a line-of-battle ship, as she
launched herself in long floating
rushes from gleaming pinnacle to
seething valley with a heavy, melancholy sobbing of water all about her
decks, and her narrow, distended
band of maintopsail hovering over-

head black as a raven's pinion in the
flying hoariness. We were washing
through it at twelve or thirteen knots
an hour, though the ship was as stiff
as a madman in a strait-jacket, with
the compressed wool in her hold and
loaded down to her main-chain bolts
besides. By two bells (one o'clock)
forward of the break of the poop the
decks were deserted, though now and
again, amidst some swiftly passing
flaw in the storm of snow, you might
just discern the gleaming shapes of
two men on the look-out on the forecastle, with the glimpse of a figure in
the foretop, also on the watch for
anything that might be ahead. The
captain in his tall hat was stumping
the deck to and fro close against the
wheel, cased in a long pilot coat,
under the skirts of which his legs, as
he slewed round, showed like the
lower limb of the letter O. Through
the closed skylight windows I could
get a sort of watery view of the cuddy
passengers—as they were then called
—reading, playing at chess, playing
the piano, below. There were some
scores of steerage and 'tween-deck
passengers, deeper yet in the bowels
of the ship, but hidden out of sight
by the closed hatches.

I know not why it should have
been, but I was the only midshipman

on the poop, though the ship carried
twelve of us, six to a watch. The other
five were doubtless loafing about under cover somewhere. I stood close
beside the chief mate to windward,
holding to the brass rail that ran
athwart the break of the poop. This
officer was a Scotchman, a man
named Thompson, and I suppose no
better seaman ever trod a ship's deck.
He was talking to me about getting
home, asking me whether I would
rather be off Cape Horn in a snow-
storm or making ready to sit down
with my brothers and sisters at my
father's table to a jolly good dinner
of fish and roast beef and pudding,
when all on a sudden he stopped in
what he was saying, and fell a-sniffing
violently.

"I smell ice," said he, with a
glance aft at the captain.

"Smell ice!" thought I, with a half
look at him, for I believed he was
joking. For my part, it was all ice
to me—one dense, yelling atmosphere of snow ; every flake barbed,
and the cold of a bitterness beyond
words. He fell a-sniffing again,
quickly and vehemently, and stepped
to the side, sending a thirsty look into
the white blindness ahead, whilst I
heard him mutter, "There's ice close
aboard, there's ice close aboard!"

As he spoke the words, there arose a loud and fearful cry from the fore-castle.

"Ice right ahead, sir!"

"Ice right ahead, sir!" repeated the chief mate, whipping round upon the captain.

"I see it, sir!" I see it, sir!" roared the skipper. "Hard a starboard, men! Hard a starboard for your lives! Over with it!"

The two fellows at the helm sent the spokes flying like the driving-wheel of a locomotive; the long ship, upborne at the instant by a huge Pacific sea, paid off like a creature of instinct, sweeping slowly but surely to port just in time. For right on the starboard bow of us there leapt out into proportions terrible and magnificent, within a musket shot of our rail, an iceberg that looked as big as St. Paul's Cathedral, with stormy roaring of the gale in its ravines and valleys, and the white smoke of the snow revolving about its pinnacles and spires like volumes of steam, and a volcanic noise of mighty seas bursting against its base and recoiling from the adamant of its crystalline sides in acres of foam. We were heading for it at the rate of thirteen miles an hour as neatly as you point the end of a thread into the eye of a needle.

In a few minutes we should have been into it, crumbled against it, dissolved upon the white waters about it, and have met a nameless end. Boy as I was, and bitter as was the day, I remember feeling a stir in my hair as I stood watching with open mouth the passage of the mountainous mass close alongside into the pale void astern, whilst the ship trembled again to the blows and thumps of vast blocks of floating ice.

"Ice right ahead, sir!" came the cry again, nor could we clear the jumble of bergs until the dusk had settled down, when we hove-to for the night. No one was hurt, but I suppose no closer shave of the kind ever happened to a ship before.

Again, and this time once more off Cape Horn. It was my third voyage; I was still a midshipman, and in the second mate's watch. I came on deck at midnight and found the ship hove-to, breasting what in this age of steamboats, and, for the matter of that, perhaps in any other age, might be termed a terrific sea. She was making good weather of it—that is to say, she kept her decks dry, but she was diving and rolling most hideously, with such swift headlong shearing of her spars through the gale that the noises up in the blackness aloft were

5

as though the spirits of the inmates
of a thousand lunatic asylums had
been suddenly enlarged from their
bodies and sent yelling into limbo.
The wind blew with an unendurable
edge in the sting and bite of it. The
second mate and I, each with a rope
girdling his waist to swing by, stood
muffled up to our noses under the lee
of a square of canvas seized to the
mizzen shrouds. Presently he roared
into my ear, " Sort of a night for a
pannikin of coffee, eh, Mr. Russell ? "
" Ay, ay, sir," I replied, and with
that, liberating myself from the rope,
I clawed my way along the line of
the hencoops—the decks sometimes
sloping almost up and down to the
heavy weather *scends* of the huge
black billows,—and descended into
the midshipmen's berth. It was not
the first time I had made a cup of
coffee for myself and the second
mate in the middle watch during cold
weather. An old nurse who had
lived in my family for years had
given me an apparatus consisting of
a spirit-lamp and a funnel-shaped
contrivance of block tin, along with
several pounds of very good coffee,
and with this I used to keep the
second mate and myself supplied
with the real luxury of a hot and
aromatic drink during wet and frosty

watches. The midshipmen's berth
was a narrow room down in the
'tween decks, bulkheaded off from
the sides, fitted with a double row of
bunks, one on top of another, the
lower beds being about a foot above
the deck. There were five midshipmen all turned in and fast asleep.
The others, who were on watch,
were clustered under the break of
the poop for the shelter there. A
lonely one-eyed sort of slush lamp,
with sputtering wick and stinking
flame, swung wearily from a blackened
beam, rendering the darkness but little more than visible. I slung my little
cooking apparatus near to it, filled
the lamp with spirits of wine, put
water and coffee into the funnel, and
then set fire to the arrangement. I
stood close under it, wrapped from
head to foot in gleaming oilskins—
looking a very bloated little shape, I
don't doubt, from the quantity of
clothing I wore under the waterproofs,
—waiting for the water to boil. The
seas roared in thunder high above
the scuttles to the wild and sickening
dipping of the ship's side into the
trough. The humming of the gale
pierced through the decks with the
sound of a crowd of bands of music
in the distance, all playing together
and each one a different tune. The

midshipmen snored, and coats and smallclothes hanging from the bunk stanchions wearily swung sprawling out and in, like bodies dangling from gallows in a gale of wind.

All in a moment a sea of unusual weight and fury took the ship and hove her down to the height as you would have thought, of her top-gallant rail ; the headlong movement sent me sliding to leeward ; the fore-thatch of my sou'wester struck the spirit-lamp ; down it poured, in a line of fire upon the deck, where it surged to and fro in a sheet of flame, with the movements of the ship. I was so horribly frightened as to be almost paralysed by the sight of that flicker-ing stretch of yellowish light, spark-ling and leaping as it swept under the lower bunks and came racing back again to the bulkhead with the windward incline. I fell to stamping upon it in my sea-boots, little fool that I was, hoping in that way to ex-tinguish it. A purple-faced midship-man occupied one of the lower bunks, and his long nose lay over the edge of it. He opened his eyes, and after looking sleepily for a moment or two at the coating of pale fire rushing from under his bed, he snuffed a bit, and muttering, " Doocid nice smell ; burnt brandy, ain't it ?" he turned over and went to sleep again with his face the other way.

I was in an agony of consternation, and yet afraid of calling for help lest I should be very roughly manhandled for my carelessness. There was a deal of "raffle" under the bunks—sea-boots, little bundles of clothing, and I know not what else ; but thanks to Cape Horn everything was happily as damp as water itself. There was therefore nothing to kindle, nor was there any aperture through which the burning spirit could run below into the hold ; so by degrees the flaming stuff consumed itself, and in about ten minutes' time the planks were black again. I went on deck and re-ported what had happened to the second mate. All he said was "My God!" and instantly ran below to satisfy himself that there was no fur-ther danger. I can never recall that little passage of my life without a shudder. There were a hundred and ninety-five souls of us aboard, and had I managed to set the ship on fire that night the doom of every living creature would have been assured, seeing that no boat could have lived an instant in such a sea as was then running.

In a very different climate from that of Cape Horn I came very near

to meeting with an extremely ugly
end.   It was a little business entirely
out of the routine of the ordinary
ocean dangers, but the memory of it
sends a thrill through me to this hour,
though it is much past twenty years
ago since it happened.   I was making my second voyage aboard a small
full-rigged ship that had been hired
by the Government for the convey-
ance of troops to the East Indies.   I
was the only midshipman ; the other
youngsters consisted of five apprentices.   We occupied a deck-house a
little forward of the main-hatch.
This house was divided by a fore and
aft bulkhead ; the apprentices lived
in the port compartment, the third
and fourth mates and myself slung
our hammocks on the starboard side.
The third mate was a man of good
family, aged about twenty-one, a
young Hercules in strength, with
heavy under-jaws and the low, peculiar brow of the prize-fighter.   He
had been a midshipman in Smith's
service, and was a good and active
sailor, very nimble aloft and expert
in his work about the ship, but of a
sullen, morose disposition, and a
heavy drinker whenever the opportunity to get drink presented itself.   I
think he was regarded by all hands
as a little touched, but I was too

young to remark in him any oddities
which might strike an older observer.
He was given to delivering himself of
certain dark, wild fancies. I remember he once told me that if he owed
a man a grudge he would not scruple
to plant himself alongside of him on
a yard on a black night and kick the
foot-rope from under him when his
hands were busy, and so let him go
overboard. But this sort of talk I
would put down to mere boasting,
and indeed I thought nothing of it.

We were in the Indian Ocean, and
one evening I sat at supper (as tea,
the last meal on board ship, is always
called) along with this man and the
fourth mate. We fell into some sort
of nautical argument, and in the heat
of the discussion I said something
that caused the third mate to look at
me fixedly for a little while, whilst he
muttered under his breath, in a kind
of half-stifled way, as though his teeth
were set. I did not catch the words,
but I am quite certain from the fourth
mate's manner, that he had heard
them, and that he knew what was in
the other's mind. I say this because
I recollect that very shortly afterwards the fellow rose and walked out
on deck with an air about him as if
he was willing to give the third mate
a chance of being alone with me. It

was a mean trick, but then he was a
cowardly rogue, and when I afterwards heard that he had been dis-
missed from the service he had
formerly entered for robbing his
shipmates of money and tobacco and
the humble trifles which sailors carry
about with them in their sea-chests I
was wicked enough, recalling how he
had walked out of that deck-house,
leaving me, a little boy, alone with a
strong, brutal, crazy third mate, to
hope that he might yet prove guilty
of larger sins still, for I could not but
regard him as a creature that deserved to be hanged. The instant
this man stepped through the door
the third mate jumped up and closed
it. It travelled in grooves, and he
whipped it to with a temper which
caused the whole structure to echo
again to the blow.

"Now, you young ——" he exclaimed, turning his bull-dog face,
white with rage, upon me, yet speaking in a cold voice that was more
terrifying to listen to than if he had
roared out, "I have you and I mean
to punish you," and with that he un-
clasped his heavy belt, and then
clasped it again so as to make a double thong of the leather, and grasped
me by the collar.

What my feelings were I am unable

to state at this distance of time. I
believe I was more astonished than
frightened. I could not imagine that
this huge creature was in earnest in
offering to beat me for what I had
said, and yet I was sensible too of an
unnatural fire in his eyes—a glow that
put an expression of savage exulta-
tion into them ; and this look of his
somehow held me motionless and
speechless. He half raised his arm,
but a sudden irresolution possessed
him, as though my passivity was a
check upon his intentions.

"No, no," he exclaimed, after a
little, " I 'll manage better than this " ;
and still grasping me by the collar of
my jacket he dropped his belt and
ran me to the fore end of the compartment, threw me on my back, and
knelt upon me. Within reach of his
arm, kneeling as he was, were three
shelves on which we kept such crock-
ery and cutlery as we owned, along
with our slender stores of sugar and
flour and the cold remains of previous repasts. He felt for a knife; I
could hear the blades rattle as his
fingers groped past his curved wrist
for one of them, and then flourishing
the black-handled weapon in front of
my eyes he exclaimed, " Now I'm
going to murder you." I lay stock-
still ; I never uttered a word ; I

scarcely breathed indeed. Again, I
say that I do not know that I was
terrified. My condition was one of
semi-stupefaction, I think, with just
enough of sense left in me to com-
prehend that if I uttered the least cry
or struggled, no matter how faintly, I
should transform him into a wild
beast. Nothing but my lying corpse-
like under the pressure of his knee
saved me, I am certain. My gaze
was fixed upon his face, and I see him
now staring at me with his little eyes
on fire, and the knife poised ready to
plunge. This posture maybe he re-
tained for two or three minutes ; it
ran into long hours to me. Then on
a sudden he threw the knife away
backwards over his shoulder, rose
and went to the door, where he stood
a little staring at me intently. I continued to lie motionless. He opened
the door and passed out, on which I
sprang to my feet and fled as nimbly
as my legs would carry me to the
poop, where I found the chief mate.
He was a little Welshman of the name
of Thomas, a brother of Ap Thomas,
the celebrated harpist, and if he be
still alive and these lines should meet
his eyes, let him be pleased to know
that my memory holds him in cordial
respect as the kindest officer and the
smartest seaman I ever had the for-

tune to be shipmates with. To him I
related what had happened.

"O—ho," cried he, "attempted
murder, hey? Our friend must be
taught that we don't allow this sort of
thing to happen aboard *us*."

He gave certain orders and shortly
afterwards the third mate was seized
and locked up in a spare cabin just
under the break of the poop. Two
powerful seamen were told off to
keep him company. How much the
unfortunate man needed this sort of
control I could not have imagined
but for my hearing that he was locked
up and my going to the cabin window that looked on to the quarter
deck to take a peep at him if he was
visible. He saw me and bounded to
the window, bringing his leg-of-mut-
ton fist against it with a blow that
crashed the whole plate of glass into
splinters. His face was purple, his
eyes half out of their sockets. There
was froth upon his lips, with such a
general distortion of features that it
would be impossible to figure a more
horrible illustration of madness than
his countenance. I bolted as if the
devil had been after me, catching just
a glimpse of the powerful creature
wrestling in the grasp of the two seamen who were dragging him backwards into the gloom of the cabin.

Such an escape as this I regard as distinctly more eventful, if not more romantic, than falling overboard and being rescued when almost spent, or being picked up after a fortnight's exposure in an open boat. My most sleep-murdering nightmares nearly always include the phantom form of that burly, crazed third mate kneeling upon my motionless little figure and feeling for a knife on one of the shelves just over my head.

Another little plum out of my plain sailor's pudding. This time my ship was an East Indian trader that whilst lying at Calcutta was chartered by the Government to convey troops to the North of China. It was in 1860. Difficulties had arisen, and John Chinaman was to be attacked. We proceeded to Hong Kong with the headquarters of the 60th Rifles on board, and thence to the Gulf of Pe-che-li, which I should say submitted one of the finest spectacles in the world, with its congregations of transports and English and French and Yankee ships of war. It was an old-world scene which the sponge of time has obliterated for ever, and I behold again in memory those two noble frigates, the *Impérieuse* and the *Chesapeake*, straining tightly at their cables, with smoke-stacks too modest

in proportions to impair to the critical nautical eye the tack and sheet
suggestions of the graceful, exqui-
sitely symmetrical fabric of spars
and yards and rigging soaring trium-
phantly aloft to where the long whip
or pennant at the main flickered like a
delicate line of fire against the hard
cold blue of the Asiatic sky.

We lay for many months in that
bay, and were obliged repeatedly to
send ashore for fresh meat, vegetables,
and the like. On one occasion I recollect going with the mate in the
long-boat some distance up the river
Peiho, a rushing, turbid stream at the
mouth of which the Chinese had
fixed a very *chevaux-de-frise* of spikes,
upon which they had fondly hoped
our men-of-war would impale themselves, forgetting that the depth of
water scarcely permitted the approach
of a shallow gunboat. We were
returning to the ship with a fair wind,
and on top of the fierce rush of the
river, when our helmsman run us
plump against one of Johnny's huge
impalers. The shock of the blow
threw the mate into an immense
basket of fresh eggs. He fell with a
squelch past all power of forgetting,
and lay wriggling in a very quagmire
of yolk and white and fragments of
shells. We pulled him out blind and

streaming with eggs. His aspect was
so preposterously absurd that the
helmsman, rendered almost imbecile
by laughter, let the boat drive into a
second pile, when, as I live to write
it, the mate, who was cleaning himself near to the basket, was thrown a
second time into the glutinous mess !
I will not attempt to repeat the sea-
blessings he bestowed upon the steers-
man. Happily eggs were cheap, and
a dollar might have represented a
more considerable smash. Now it
was two days following this that the
captain sent the long-boat to procure
some sheep and poultry from a little
village situated close to the shores of
the bay on the north of the river.
The second mate took charge, and I
and another midshipman and a
couple of sailors went along with
him. We landed and left the boat in
charge of a seaman, and strolled
towards the village. The second
mate was a wild, dissolute young
fellow, who, before he quitted China,
became the recipient of more than one
round dozen by order of the provost-
marshal for looting. A little knot of
Chinamen stood watching as we
approached, whilst just beyond we
caught sight of a couple of women
hobbling nimbly away out of reach of
our sight, as though they walked on

stilts. Sherman—for such was the second mate's name,--approaching the Chinamen, began with them in pigeon English. They did not understand. He exhibited a few dollars, and traced the outline of a sheep upon the ground, and, with many surprising motions of his arms, sought to acquaint them with the object of his visit. All to no purpose. "What 's to be done?" said Sherman, looking at us. "There 's nothing that resembles a sheep hereabouts." His eyes suddenly brightened as they lighted on a large concourse of cocks and hens pecking in tolerably close order at some fifty paces distant from us. "Boys," he shouted, "as these chaps can't be made to understand, let 's help ourselves. Each one seize what he can get and make for the boat. Follow me." He sprang with incredible agility towards the fowls, and in a trice had a couple of them shrieking and fluttering in his grasp. In a breath the Chinamen—thirty or forty strong—uttering a long, peculiar shout, armed themselves with pitch-forks—at all events, a species of weapon that to my young eyes re-sembled a pitchfork,—sticks, and stones, and gave chase. They tramped after us with the noise of an

army in pursuit. We flew towards
the boat, screaming to the fellow in
charge to haul in and receive us. A
stone struck me in the small of my
back, and urged me forwards faster
than my legs were travelling. Down I
should have tumbled on my nose, and
in that posture have been straightway
massacred, but for the timely grip of a
sailor who was running by my side.
" Hold up, my hearty ! " he roared,
hooking his fingers into the back of
my collar and jerking me backwards.
In a few moments we gained the boat,
wading waist-high to come at her, and
rolling like drunken men over her
gunwale into her bottom. A volley
of stones rattled about our ears, but
we were safe. Had the Chinamen
carried firearms, not one of us but
must have been shot down.

I could relate a score or more of
such experiences : of ugly collisions
with the police in Calcutta, of a narrow escape of being thrown overboard by a dinghy-wallah of the river
Hooghley, of a desperate fight in the
slings of the mizzen-topgallant yard
with an apprentice of my own age,
and the like ; but the space at my
disposal obliges me to conclude.
Very little of the heroic enters the
sailor's life. The risks he runs, the
adventures he encounters, have, as a

rule, nothing of the romantic in them ;
they are mainly brought about by
his own foolhardiness, by the pro-
verbial carelessness that is utterly
irreconcilable with the stern obliga-
tions of vigilance, alertness, and fore-
sight imposed upon him by the
nature of his calling, by the imbe-
cility of shipmates, and much too
often by drink. Yet no matter what
the cause of most of the perils he
meets with, his experiences, I take it,
head the march of professional dangers. Small wonder that faith in the
"sweet little cherub that sits up
aloft" should still linger in the forecastle. For certainly were it not for
the bright look-out kept over him by
some sort of maritime angel, the
mariner would rank foremost as
amongst the most perishable of human products.

6

The Strange Adventures of a South Seaman.

ON November 4th, 1830, a number of convicts were indicted at the Admiralty Sessions of the Old Bailey for having on the 5th of September in the previous year piratically seized a brig called the *Cyprus*. A South Seaman was innocently and most involuntarily, as shall be discovered presently, involved in this tragic business, to which he is able to add a narrative that is certainly not known to any of the chroniclers of crime. But first as to the piratical seizure.

The *Cyprus*, a colonial brig, had been chartered to convey a number of convicts from Hobart Town to Macquarie Harbour, on the northern coast of Tasmania, and Norfolk Island, distant about a week's sail from Sydney · in those days a penal settlement. There were thirty-two felons

in all.   These men had been guilty
of certain grave offences at Hobart
Town, and they had rendered themselves in consequence liable to new
punishment ; they were tried before
the Supreme Court of Judicature
there, and sentenced to be transported to the place above mentioned.

Only the very worst sort of prisoners were sent to Norfolk Island and
Macquarie Harbour.   The discipline
at those penal settlements was terrible ; the labour that was exacted,
heart-breaking.   The character of
the punishment was well known, and
every felon re-sentenced to transpor-
tation from the colonial convict settlements very well understood the
fate that was before him.

The *Cyprus* sailed from Hobart
Town in August, 1829.   In addition
to the thirty-two convicts, she carried
a crew of eight men and a guard of
twelve soldiers, under the command
of Lieutenant Carew, who was accompanied by his wife and children.
The prisoners, as was always customary in convict ships, were under the
care of a medical man named Williams.

Nothing of moment happened until the brig either brought up or was
hove-to in Research Bay, where Dr.

Williams, Lieutenant Carew, the mate of the vessel, a soldier, and a convict named Popjoy went ashore on a fishing excursion. They had not been gone from the ship above half-an-hour when they heard a noise of fire-arms. Instantly guessing that the convicts had risen, they made a rush for the boat and pulled for the brig. It was as they had feared: the felons had mastered the guard and seized the brig. They suffered no man to come on board save Popjoy, who, however, later on sprang overboard, and swam to the beach. They then sent the crew, soldiers, and passengers ashore, but without provisions and the means of supporting life. Then, amongst themselves, the prisoners lifted the anchor and trimmed sail, and the little brig slipped away out of Research Bay.

The chroniclers state that the vessel was never afterward heard of, though some of the convicts were apprehended, separately, in various parts of Sussex and Essex. The posthumous yarn of the mate of an English whaler disproves this. He relates his extraordinary experience thus :

" We had been fishing north of the Equator, and had filled up with a little 'grease,' as the Yankees term it,

round about the Galapagos Islands,
but business grew too slack for even a
whaleman's patience. Eleven months
out from Whitby, and, if my memory
fails me not, less than a score of full
barrels in our hold ! So the Captain
made up his mind to try south, and
working our way across the Equator,
we struck in amongst the Polynesian
groups, raising the Southern Cross
higher and higher, till we were somewhere about latitude 30 deg., and longitude 175 deg. E.

" I came on deck to the relief
at four o'clock one morning : the
weather was quiet, a pleasant breeze
blowing off the starboard beam ; our
ship was barque-rigged, with short,
topgallantmasts—Cape Horn fashion;
she was thrusting through it leisurely
under topsails and a maintopgallant-
sail, and the whole Pacific heave so
cradled her as she went that she
seemed to sleep as she sailed.

" Day broke soon after five, and as
the light brightened out I caught
sight of a gleam on the edge of the
sea. It was as white with the risen
sun upon it as an iceberg. I levelled the glass and made out the topmast canvas of a small vessel. There
was nothing to excite one in the
spectacle of a distant sail. The
barque's work went on ; the decks

were washed down, the look-out aloft
hailed and nothing reported, and at
seven bells the crew went to breakfast, at which hour we had risen the
distant sail with a rapidity that somewhat puzzled the captain and me.
For, first of all, she was not so far off
now but that we could distinguish the
lay of her head. She looked to be
going our way, but clearly she was
stationary, for the *Swan*, which was
the name of our barque, though as
seaworthy an old tub as ever went to
leeward on a bowline, was absolutely
without legs : nothing more sluggish
was ever afloat ; for *her* then to have
overhauled anything that was actually
under way would have been marvellous.

"'Something wrong out there,
Grainger?' said the captain.

"'Looks to me to be all in the
wind with her,' I answered.

"'Make out any colour?' said the
captain.

"'Nothing as yet,' said I.

"'Shift your helm by a spoke or
two,' said he. 'Meanwhile, I'll go
to breakfast.'

"He was not long below. By the
time he returned we had risen the
distant vessel to the line of her rail.
I got some breakfast in the cabin ;
on passing again through the hatch

I found the captain looking at the sail through the telescope.

"'She is a small brig,' said he, 'and she has just sent the English colours aloft with the jack down. She is all in the wind, as you said. Her people don't seem to know what to do with her.'

"She now lay plain enough to the naked sight ; a small black brig of about a hundred and eighty tons, apparently in ballast as she floated high on the water. She, like ourselves, carried short topgallantmasts, but the canvas she showed consisted of no more than topsails and courses. I took the glass from the captain, and believed I could make out the heads of two or three people showing above the bulwark rail abaft the mainmast.

"'What 's their trouble going to prove?' said the captain.

"'They 're waiting for us,' said I. 'They saw us, and put the helm down, and got their little ship in irons instead of backing their topsail yard. No sailor-man there, I doubt.'

"'A small colonial trader, you 'll find,' said the captain, 'with a crew of four or five Kanakas. The captain 's sick and the mate was accidentally left ashore at the last island.'

"It blew a four-knot breeze—four

knots, I mean, for the *Swan*. Wrinkling the water under her bows, and smoothing into oil a cable's length of wake astern of her, the whaler floated down to the little brig within hailing distance. We saw but two men, and one of them was at the wheel. There was an odd look of confusion aloft, or rather let me describe it as a want of that sort of precision which a sailor's eye would seek for and instantly miss, even in the commonest old sea-donkey of a collier. Nothing was rightly set for the lack of hauling taut. Running gear was slackly belayed, and swung with the rolling of the little brig like Irish pennants. The craft was clean at the bottom, but uncoppered. She was a round-bowed contrivance, with a spring aft which gave a kind of mulish, kick-up look to the run of her.

"One of the two visible men, a broad-chested, thick-set fellow, in a black coat and a wide, white straw hat, got upon the bulwark, and stood holding on by a back-stay, watching our approach, but he did not offer to hail. I thought this queer; it struck me that he hesitated to hail us, as though wanting the language of the sea in this business of speaking.

"'Brig ahoy!' shouted the captain.

"'Hallo!' answered the man.

"'What is wrong with you?'

"'We are short-handed, sir, and in great distress,' was the answer.

"'What is your ship, and where are you from, and where are you bound to?'

"When these questions were put the man looked round to the fellow who stood at the brig's little wheel. It was certain he was not a sailor, and it was possible he sought for counsel from the helmsman, who was probably a forecastle hand. He turned his face again our way in a minute, and shouted out in a powerful voice:

"'We are the brig *Cyprus*, of Sydney, New South Wales, bound to the Cape of Good Hope, and very much out of our reckoning, I dare say, through the distress we're in.'

"The captain and I exchanged looks.

"'Heading as you go,' the captain sang out, 'you're bound on a true course for the Antarctic Circle, and, anyway, it's a long stretch for Agulhas by way of Cape Horn out of these seas. How can we serve you?'

"'Will you send one of your officers in a boat?' came back the reply very promptly, 'that he may put us in the way of steering a course for

the Cape of Good Hope? He 'll
then guess our plight, and if you 'll
lend us a hand or two we shall be
greatly obliged. We can't send a
boat ourselves—we 're too few.'

"' He 's no sailor-man, that fellow,'
said the captain, 'and he ha'n't got
the colonial brogue, either. I seem
to smell Whitechapel in that chap's
speech. Is he a passenger? Why
don't he say so? Looks like a play-
actor, or a priest. But take a boat,
Grainger, and row over and see what
you can make of the mess they 're in.
There 's something rather more than
out-of-the-way in that job, if I 'm not
mistaken.'

"A boat was lowered; I entered
it, and was rowed across to the brig
by three men. No attempt was made
to throw us the end of a line, or in
any way to help us. The bowman
got hold of a chain plate, and I
scrambled into the main-chains and
so got over the rail, bidding the men
shove off and lie clear of the brig,
whose rolling was somewhat heavy,
owing to her floating like an egg-shell
upon the long Pacific heave.

"I glanced along the vessel's decks
forward, and saw not a soul. I observed a little caboose, the chimney
of which was smoking as though coal
had within the past few minutes been

thrown into the furnace. I saw but
one boat; she stood chocked and
lashed abaft the caboose—a clumsy,
broad-beamed long-boat, capable of
stowing perhaps fifteen or twenty
men at a pinch. I also took notice
of a pair of davits on the starboard
side, past the main rigging; they
were empty.

"I stepped up to the heavily-built
man who had answered the captain's
questions. He received me with a
grotesque bow, pinching the brim of
his wide straw hat as he bobbed his
head. I did not like his looks. He
had as hanging a face as ever a male-
factor carried. His features were
heavy and coarse, his brow low and
protruding, his eyes small, black, and
restless, and his mouth of the bull-
dog cast.

"'We're much obliged to you for
this visit,' he said. 'Might I ask
your name, sir?'

"'My name is Grainger—Mr. James
Grainger,' I answered, scarcely wondering at the irregularity of such a
question on such an occasion, per-
ceiving clearly now that the fellow
was no sailor.

"'What might be your position in
that ship, Mr. Grainger?' said the
man.

"'I'm mate of her,' said I.

"'Then I suppose you're capable of carrying a ship from place to place by the art of navigation?' he exclaimed.

"'Why, I hope so!' cried I. 'But what is it you want?' and here I looked at the man who was standing at the helm, grasping the spokes in a manner that assured me he was not used to that sort of work; and I was somewhat struck to observe that in some respects he was not unlike the fellow who was addressing me—that is to say, he had quite as hanging a face as his companion, though he wanted the other's breadth and squareness, and ruffian-like set of figure; but his forehead was low, and his eyes black and restless, and he was close-cropped, with some days' growth of beard, as was the case with the other. He was dressed in a bottle-green spencer and trousers of a military cut, and wore one of those caps which in the days I am writing of were the fashion amongst masters and mates.

"'If you don't mind stepping into the cabin,' said the man with whom I was conversing, 'I'll show you a chart, and ask you to pencil out a course for us; and with your leave, sir, I'll tell you over a glass of wine exactly how it's come about that we're too few to carry the brig to her destination unless your captain will kindly help us.'

"'Are you two the only people aboard?' said I.

"'The only people,' he answered.

"Anywhere else, under any other conditions, I might have suspected a treacherous intention in two men with such hanging countenances as this lonely brace owned; but what could I imagine to be afraid of aboard a brig holding two persons only, with the whaler's boat and three men within a few strokes of the oar, and the old barque, *Swan*, full of livelies, many of them deadly in the art of casting the harpoon, within easy hail?

"The man who invited me below stepped into the companion-way; I followed and descended the short flight of steps. The instant I had gained the bottom of the ladder I knew by the sudden shadow which came into the light that the companion hatch had been closed; this must have been done by the fellow who was standing at the wheel. It was wisely contrived. Assuredly had the way been open, I should have rushed upon deck and sprung overboard: because after descending the steps I beheld five or six men standing in a sort of waiting and listening posture under the skylight. Instantly my left arm was gripped by the man who had asked me to step below, while another fellow, equally powerful, and equally ruffianly in appearance, grasped me by the right arm.

"'Now,' said the first man, 'if you make the least bit of noise or give us any trouble, we'll cut your throat. We don't intend to do you any harm, but we want your services, and you'll have to do what we require without any fuss. If not, you're a dead man.'

"So saying, they threw open the door of a berth, ran me into it, shut the door, and shot the lock. I had been so completely taken by surprise that I was in a manner stunned. I stood in the middle of the cabin just where the fellows had let go of me, staring around, breathing short and fierce, my mind almost a blank. But I quickly rallied my wits. I understood I had been kidnapped; by what sort of people I could not imagine, but beyond question because I understood navigation, as I had told the man. I listened, but heard no noise of voices, nor movements of people in the cabin. Through the planks, overhead, however, came the sound of a rapid tread of feet, accompanied by the thud of coils of rope flung hastily down. The cabin porthole was a middling-sized, circular window. I saw the whaler in it as in a frame. I unscrewed the port, but with no intention to cry out, never doubting for a moment from the looks of the men that they would silence me in some bloody fashion as had been threatened.

"Just as I pulled the port open a voice overhead sang out : 'Get back to your ship, you three men ; your mate has consented to stop with us as we 're in want of a navigator.'

"'Let him tell us that himself,' said one of my men ; 'let him show up. What ha' ye done with him ?'

"'Be off,' roared one of the people, in a savage, hurricane note.

"There was a little pause as of astonishment on the part of the boat's crew—I could not see them, the boat lay too far astern,—but after a bit I heard the splash of oars, the boat swept into the sphere of the porthole, and I beheld her making for the barque.

"I was now sensible, however, not only by observing the whaler to recede, but by hearing the streaming and rippling of broken waters along the bends, that the people of the brig had in some fashion trimmed

sail and filled upon the vessel. We
were under way. The barque slided
out of the compass of the porthole.
but now I heard her captain's voice
coming across the space of water,
clear and strong :

" ' Brig ahoy ! What do you mean
by keeping my mate ? '

" To this no answer was returned.
Again the captain hailed the brig ;
but owing to the shift in the postures
of the two vessels, and to my having
nothing but a circular hole to hear
through, I could only dimly and im-
perfectly catch what was shouted.
The cries from the whaler grew more
and more threadlike. Indeed, I knew
the brig must be a very poor sailer if
she did not speedily leave the *Swan*
far astern.

" And now, as I conjectured from
the noise of the tread of feet and the
hum of voices, the brig on a sudden
seemed full of men ; not the eight or
ten whom I had beheld with my own
eyes, but a big ship's company. And
the sight of the crowd, I reckoned,
as I stood hearkening at the open
porthole — amazed, confounded, in
the utmost distress of mind—was
probably the reason why the captain
of the *Swan* had not thought proper
to send boats to rescue me. Be this
as it will I was thunderstruck by the

discovery—the discovery of my hearing, and of my capacity as a sailor of
interpreting shipboard sounds—that
this little brig, which I had supposed
tenanted by two men only, had hidden
a whole freight of human souls somewhere away in the execution of this
diabolical stratagem. What was this
vessel? Who were the people on
board her? What use did they
design to put me to? And when I
had served them, what was to be my
fate?

"Quite three hours passed, during
which I was left unvisited. Sometimes I heard men talking in the
cabin; over my head there went a
regular swing of heavy feet, a pendu-
lum tread, as of half-a-score of burly
ruffians marching abreast, and keeping a look-out all together. The
door of my berth was opened at last,
and the villain who had seduced me
into the brig stepped in.

"'I was sorry,' said he, 'to be
obliged to use threats. Threats
are n't in our way. We mean no
mischief. Quite the contrary; we
count upon you handsomely serving
us. Come into the cabin, sir, that I
may make you known to my mates.'

"His manner was as civil as a fellow with his looks could possibly
contrive, and an ugly smile sat upon

7

his face whilst he addressed me, and I observed that he held his great straw hat in his hand, as though to show respect.

"About twenty men were assembled in the cabin. I came to a dead stand on the threshold of the door of the berth, so astounded was I by the sight of all those fellows. I ran my eye swiftly over them; they were variously dressed—some in the attire of seamen, some in such clothes as gentlemen of that period wore, a few in a puzzling sort of military undress. They all had cropped heads, and many were grim with a few days' growth of beard and moustache. They had the felon's look, and there was somehow a suggestion of escaped prisoners in their general bearing. A dark suspicion rushed upon me with the velocity of thought, as I stood on the threshold of the door of the berth for the space of a few heart-beats, gazing at the mob.

"The cabin was a plain, old-fashioned interior. A stout, wide table secured to stanchions ran amidships. Overhead was a skylight. There were a few chairs on either hand the table, and down the cabin on both sides went a length of lockers. Some of the men were smoking. A few sat upon the table with their arms folded ; others lounged upon the lockers, and in chairs. They stared like one man at me, whilst I stood looking at them.

"'Is he a navigator, Swallow?' said one of them—a wiry, dark-faced man, who held his head hung, and looked at you by lifting his eyes.

"'Ay, mate of the whaler—James Grainger by name,' answered the fellow who had opened the door of my berth. 'Salute him, bullies. He's the charley-pitcher for to handle this butter-box.'

"The voices of the men swelled into a roar of welcomes of as many sorts as there were speakers. One of them came round the table and shook me by the hand.

"'My name's Alexander Stevenson,' said he ; 'come and sit you down here.'

"All very civilly he conducted me to a chair at the head of the table. And now, happening to glance upwards, I spied seven or eight faces peering down at me through the skylight.

"'Swallow, do the jawing, will 'ee?' said the man who called himself Stevenson.

"'Why, yes,' answered Swallow, posting himself at the top of the table, and addressing me through the

double ranks of men on either side.
'This is how it stands with us, Mr.
Grainger—clear as mud in a wineglass; and we 're sorry it should
have come to it, for your sake. But
do your duty by us faithfully, and
we 'll take care you sha' n't suffer.
We 're thirty-one convicts in all.
We were thirty-two, but Milkliver
Poppy took a header, and went for
the land and the lickspittle; if he
lives he 'll get his liberty for a reward.
We were bound from Hobart to Norfolk Island. You 'll have heard of
that settlement?'

" I said 'Yes,' and an odd guttural
laugh broke from some of the men.

"' Well, mister,' continued the man
Swallow, ' Norfolk Island was a destination that did n't accord with our
views. And what more d' ye want
me to say? Here we are, and we
want our liberty, and we mean to get
it without any risk, and you 're the
man to help us.'

"' What do you want me to do?'
said I, speaking boldly, and looking
about me steadily, for now I perceived exactly how it was with the
brig, and the worst had been explained and the whole mystery
solved when Swallow told me they
were convicts; and likewise I had
plenty of time to screw my nerves up.

" Several men spoke at once on my asking the above question. Stevenson roared out : 'Let Swallow man the jaw tackle, boys. One at a time, or you 'll addle the gent.'

" ' This is what we want you to do,' said Swallow. 'There are scores of islands in these seas, and we want you to carry us to them ; heaving-to off them one after another that we may pick and choose, some going ashore here, and some there, for our game is to scatter. That 's clear, I hope.'

" ' I understand you,' said I."

"Swallow seemed at a loss. Stevenson then said : 'But we shall want nothing that 's got a white settlement on it ; nothing that 's likely to have a pennant flying near. We 've got no fixed notions. We leave it to you to raise the islands, and it 'll be for us to select and take our chance.'

" ' There 'll be charts aboard, I suppose ?' said I.

" Instantly one of them stepped into a cabin and returned with a bag full of charts. I turned them out upon the table and promptly came across charts of the North and South Pacific oceans. These charts gave me from the Philippines to Cape St. Lucas, and from the Eastern Australian coast to away as far as 120 deg. W. longitude. The men did not utter a word whilst I looked ; I could hear their deep breathing, mingled with the noise of a hard sucking of pipes. One of them who looked through the skylight called down. Swallow silenced him with a gesture of his fist.

" ' Have you got what 's wanted here, Mr. Grainger ? ' said Stevenson.

" ' All that I shall want is here,' I answered.

" ' A low growl of applause ran through the men.

" ' Will you be able to light upon the islands that 'll prove suitable for us men to live on without risk until the opportunity comes in the shape of vessels for us to get away ? ' said Swallow.

" ' I 'll do my best for you,' said I. ' I see your wants, and you may trust me, providing I may trust you. What 's to become of me when you 're out of the brig ? That 's it ! '

" ' You 'll stay on board and do what you like with the vessel,' answered Swallow. ' She 'll be yours to have and hold. Make what you call a salvage job of it, and your pickings, mister, 'ull be out and away beyond the value of what we 've been obliged to make you leave behind you.'

"'Ain't that fair?' said a man.

"'Is my life safe?' said I.

"'Ay,' cried the Swallow, with a great oath, striking the table a heavy blow with his clenched fist. 'Understand this and comfort yourself. There's been no blood shed in this job, and there'll be none, so help me God—you permitting, mister.'

"When this was said, a fellow, whom I afterwards heard called by the name of Jim Davies, asked if I was willing to take an oath that I would be honest. I said, 'Yes.' He stood up and dictated an oath full of blasphemy, shocking with imprecations, and grossly illiterate. The eyes of the crowd fastened upon me, and some of the ruffians watched me in a scowling way with faces dark with suspicion, till I repeated the horrid language of the man Davies, and swore, after which the greater bulk of them went on deck.

"Swallow put some beef and biscuit on the table and a bottle of rum, and bade me fall to. He told me to understand that I was captain of the ship; that I was at liberty to appoint officers under me; and that, though none of the convicts had been seafaring men, they had learnt how the ropes led and how to furl canvas, and would obey any orders for the com-

mon good which I might deliver. I
ate and drank, being determined to
put the best face I could on this
extraordinary business, and asked for
the captain's cabin, that I might find
out what nautical instruments the
brig carried. Swallow, Stevenson,
and a convict named William Watts
conducted me to a berth right aft on
the starboard side. They told me it
had been occupied by the captain, and
should be mine. Here I found all I
needed in the shape of navigating instruments, and went on deck with
Swallow and the others.

"I could see nothing of the *Swan*;
she was out of sight from the elevation
of the brig's bulwarks. All the convicts were on deck, and the brig
looked full of men. Those who had
been above whilst I was in the cabin
with the others, approached and
stared at me, but not insolently—
merely with curiosity. They seemed
a vile lot, one and all. With some of
them every other word was an oath ;
their talk was almost gibberish to my
ears with thieves' slang. I wondered
to find not one of them dressed in
felon's garb ; but on reflection I concluded that they had plundered the
crew and the people who had had
charge of them and of the *Cyprus*, and
had forced all those they drove out

of the brig to change clothes before quitting the vessel.

"However, it was my immediate policy to prove my sincerity. I valued my life, and I had but to look at the men to reckon that it would not be worth a rushlight if they suspected I was not doing my best to find them a safe asylum among the islands in the Pacific. Accordingly, I fetched one of the charts, placed it upon the skylight, where those who gathered about me could see it, and laid off a course for the Tonga Islands; telling the men as I pointed to the group upon the chart that if no island thereabouts satisfied them, we could head for the Fijis or cruise about the Friendly or Navigator groups, working our way as far as the Low Archipelago, betwixt which and the first island we sighted we ought certainly to fall in with the sort of hiding-place they wanted. My words raised a grin of satisfaction in every face within reach of my voice.

" I stepped to the helm and headed the brig on a northerly course, and stood awhile looking at the compass to satisfy myself that the convict who grasped the spokes understood what to do with the wheel. He managed fairly well. I then asked Swallow to serve as my chief mate, and Steven-

son to act as second, and calling the
rest of the felons together, I divided
them into two watches. My next step
was to crowd the little brig with all
the canvas she could spread, and set
every stitch of it properly. Thus
passed the first day.

" I have no time to enter minutely
into what happened till we made a
small point of land in the neighbourhood of the Friendly Islands. There
was abundance of provisions on
board, plenty of fresh water, and a
stock of spirits intended for the com-
mandant and soldiers at Macquarie
Harbour and Norfolk Island ; but
though the convicts freely used whatever they found in the brig's hold,
never once was there an instance
of drunkenness amongst them. I
guessed them all to be as desperate a
set of miscreants as were ever transported for crime upon crime from a
convict establishment ; yet they used
me very well. Saving their villainous
speech, their behaviour was fairly
decorous. They sprang to my bidding, sir'd me as though they had
been seamen and I their captain, and,
indeed, by their behaviour so re-
assured me that my dread of being
butchered vanished, and I carried on
the brig as assured of my personal
safety—providing I dealt by them

honestly—as though I had been on
board the old *Swan*.

"We sighted several vessels, but,
as you may suppose, we had nothing
to say to them. Off the first island
we came across I hove the brig to ;
the convicts got the long-boat out,
and a dozen of them went ashore to
examine and report. Five returned ;
the remainder had chosen to stay.
We made three of the islands ; the
natives of two of them were threaten-
ing, and frightened the convicts back
to the brig ; the third proved unin-
habited—a very gem of an island was
this,—and here fifteen convicts went
ashore, and thrice the boat went between the island and the brig with
provisions and necessaries for their
maintenance.

"But it gave me a fortnight of
anxious hunting to discover such
another island as the remaining convicts considered suitable. This at
last we fell in with midway betwixt
the Union group and the Marquesas ;
and here the rest of the felons went
ashore, after almost emptying the
brig's hold of provisions and the like.
They kept the long-boat, and left me
alone in the brig. Some of them
shook hands with me as they went
over the side, and thanked me for
having served them so honestly.

"It was in the evening when I was left alone. The sun was setting behind the island, off which a gentle breeze was blowing. My first business was to run the ensign aloft, jack down. I then trimmed sail as best I could with my single pair of hands, and, putting the helm amidships, let the brig blow away south-west, designing to make for one of the Navigator Islands, where I might hope to fall in with assistance, either from the shore or from a vessel. But, shortly after midnight the brig, sailing quietly, grounded upon a coral shoal, fell over on to her bilge, and lay quiet. I was without a boat, and could do nothing but wait for daylight, and pray for a sight of some passing vessel. All next day passed, and nothing showed the wide horizon round; but about nine o'clock that night, the moon shining clearly, I spied a sail down in the south. She drew closer, and proved a little schooner. I hailed her with a desperate voice, and to my joy was answered, and in less than ten minutes she sent a boat and took me aboard."

The South Seaman's narrative ends abruptly here, but it is known that he was conveyed to Honolulu, at which place, strangely enough, the *Swan*

touched after he had been ashore
about a week. He at once went on
board, related his strange experiences
to his captain, and proceeded on his
whaling career with the easy indiffer-
ence of a sailor accustomed to tragic
surprises.

The brig *Cyprus* went to pieces on
the shoal on which she had grounded.
It is on record that of the convicts
retaken on their return to England,
two were hanged—namely, Watts and
Davies ; two others, Beveridge and
Stevenson, were transported for life
to Norfolk Island ; and Swallow was
sent back to Macquarie Harbour.

The Adventures of Three Sailors.

TOLD BY DANIEL SMALL, ONLY MATE.

OUR vessel was a little brig, named the *Hindoo Merchant*, and we sailed on a day in March in the year of our Lord 1857, from Trincomalee bound to Calcutta. The captain, myself, and three sailors were Europeans; the rest of the ship's company, natives. Though we were "flying light" as the term is —that is to say, though there was little more in the ship's hold than ballast, and though she had tolerably nimble heels, for what one might term a *country-wallah*—yet the little ship was so bothered with head winds and light airs, and long days of stagnation, that we had been several weeks afloat before we managed to crawl to the Norrad of the Andaman parallels, which yet left a long stretch of waters before us. If this remain-

der of the ocean was not to be tra-
versed more fleetly than the space
we had already measured, then it
was certain we should be running
short of water many a long while before the Sandheads came within the
compass of our horizon, and to pro-
vide against the most horrible situation that the crew of a ship can find
themselves placed in, we kept a
bright look-out for vessels, and within
four days managed to speak two;
but they had no water to spare, and
we pushed on.

But within three days of our speaking the second of the two vessels we
sighted a third, a large barque, who
at once backed her topsail to our sig-
nals, and hailed us to know what
we wanted. My captain, Mr. Roger
Blow, stood up in the mizzen-rigging
and asked for water. They asked
how much we needed; Captain Blow
responded that whatever they could
spare would be a god-send. On
this they sung out: "Send a boat
with a cask and you shall have
what we can afford to part with."
Captain Blow then told me to put an
eighteen-gallon cask in the port-
quarter boat, and go away to the
barque with it. "They'll not fill
it," said he, "but a half 'll be better
than a quarter, and a quarter 'll be

good enough ; for we stand to pick up more as we go along."

I had called to two of the English sailors, named Mike Jackson and Thomas Fallows, to get into the boat, when the cask had been placed in her ; and when I had entered her the darkeys lowered us ; we un-hooked and shoved off. There was a pleasant breeze of wind blowing ; it blew hot, as though it came straight from the inside of an oven, the door of which had been suddenly opened ; the sky had the sort of glazed dim-ness of the human eye in fever ; but right overhead it was of a copperish dazzle where the roasting orb of the sun was. I could not see a speck of cloud anywhere, which rendered what followed the more amazing to my mind for the suddenness of it.

The two vessels at the first of their speaking had been tolerably close to-gether, but some time had been spent in routing up the cask and getting it into the boat, and setting ourselves afloat, so that at the moment of our shoving off—spite of the topsail of each vessel being to the mast—the space had widened between them, till I daresay it covered pretty nearly a mile. The wind was at west-nor'-west, and the barque bore on the lee quarter of the *Hindoo Mer-*

chant. The great heat put a lan-
guor into the arms of our two seamen, and the oars rose and fell
slowly and weakly. Jackson said to
me : "I hope," said he, "they 'll be
able to spare us a bite of ship's bread.
Our 'n is no better than sawdust, and
if it was n't for the worms in it," said
he, "blast me if there 'd be any nutri-
ment in it at all. Them Cingalese
ought to ha' moored their island off
the Chinese coast. They 'd have
grown rich with teaching the John-
nies more tricks than they 're master
of, at plundering sailors."

"The *Hindoo Merchant's* bread
is n't up to much, Fallows," said I,
"but this is no atmosphere to talk of
bread in. What 's aboard will carry
us to the Hooghley. It is water we
have to fix our minds on."

We drew alongside of the tall
barque, and the master, after looking
over the rail, asked me to step aboard
and drink a glass with him in his
cabin, "for," says he, "this is no part
of the ocean to be thirsty in," and he
then gave directions for the cask to
be got out of the boat, and a drink of
rum and water to be handed down to
the two seamen.

I stepped into the cabin and the captain put a bottle of brandy and some
cold water on the table. He asked

8

me several questions about the brig,
and how long we were out, and where
we were from, and the like, and one
thing leading to another, he happened to mention the town he was
born in, which was my native place
too—Ashford, in the county of Kent,
—and here was now a topic to set us
yarning, for I knew some of his
friends and he knew some of mine;
and the talk seemed to do him so
much good, whilst it was so agreeable
to me, that neither of us seemed in a
hurry to end it. This is the only ex-
cuse I can offer for lingering on the
barque longer than, as circumstances
proved, I ought to have done.

At last I got up and said I must be
off, and I thanked him most kindly
for the obliging reception of me, and
for his goodness in supplying the
brig with water, and I gave him Captain Blow's compliments, and desired
to know if we could accommodate
him in any way in return. He answered "Nothing, nothing," stepping
through the hatch as he said it, and
an instant after he set up his throat
in a cry.

"You 'll have to bear a hand
aboard," says he, with a face of astonishment; "look yonder! 'T is
rolling down upon your brig like
smoke." He pointed to the vessel,

and a little way past her I spied a
long line of white vapour no higher
than Dover cliff as it looked, but as
dense as those rocks of chalk too.
The sun made steam of it, but
already it was putting a likeness of
its own blankness into the sky over
it, which seemed to be dying out, as
the vapour came along, as the light
perishes in a looking-glass upon
which you breathe.   I ran to the
side and saw my boat under the gang-
way and the two men in her.   The
cask was in the stern of the boat.
The master of the barque cried out
to me : "Will you not stay till that
smother clears?   You may lose your
brig in it."   I replied : "No, sir,
thank you.   I will take my chance.
It is more likely I should lose her by
remaining here," and with a flourish
of the hand I dropped over the side
and entered the boat.   "Now," cried
I, "pull like the devil, men."

They threw their oars over and fell
to rowing fiercely ; but the barque
was not five cables' length astern of
us when the first of the white cliff of
vapour smote the *Hindoo Merchant*,
and she vanished in it like a star in a
cloud.   There was a fresh breeze of
wind behind that line of sweeping
thickness, and in places, at the base
of the mass of blankness, it would

dart out in swift racings of shadow that made one think of the feelers of some gigantic marine spider, probing under its cobweb as though feeling its way along. In a few minutes the cloud drove down over us with a loud whistling of wind, and the water close to the boat's side ran in short, small seas, every head of it hissing ; but to within the range of a biscuit toss all was flying, glistening obscurity, with occasional bursts of denser thicknesses which almost hid one end of the boat from the other. It was about six o'clock in the afternoon, and there might be yet another hour of sunshine.

"'Vast rowing!" says I presently, "you may keep the oars over, but there's no good in pulling, short of keeping her head to wind. This is too thick to last."

"Ain't so sure of that," says Fallows, taking a slow look round at the smother, "I've been in these here seas for two days running in weather arter this pattern."

"Pity we did n't stay aboard the barque," says Jackson.

"A plague on your pities!" I cried. "I know my duty, I believe. Suppose we *had* stayed aboard the barque, we stood to be separated from the brig in this breeze and muckiness,

and was her skipper by-and-bye going
to sail in search of the *Hindoo Merchant* ? "

" A gun ! " cries Fallows.

" That 'll be the brig," says I,
catching the dull thud of the explosion of a nine-pounder which the
Hindoo Merchant carried on her
quarter-deck.

" Seems to me as though it sounded
from yonder," says Jackson, looking
away over the starboard beam of the
boat.

" What have ye there, men ? " says
I, nodding at a bundle of canvas
under the amidship thwart.

" Ship's bread," answered Jackson,
with a note of sulkiness in his voice.
" It was hove to us on my asking for
a bite. She was a liberal barque.
The cask 's more 'n three-quarters
full."

We hung upon our oars listening
and waiting. There was a second
gun ten minutes after the first had
been fired, and that was the last we
heard. The report was thin and distant, but whether ahead or astern I
could not have guessed by harkening.
I kept up my own and endeavoured
to inspirit the hearts of the others by
saying that this fog which had come
down in a moment would end in a
moment, that it was all clear sky

above with plenty of moonlight for us in the night if it should happen that the sun went down upon us thus, that Captain Blow was not going to lose us and his boat and the cask of fresh water if it was in mortal seamanship to hold a vessel in one situation ; but the fellows were not to be cheered, their spirits sank and their faces grew longer as the complexion of the fog told us that the sun was sinking fast, and I own that when it came at last to his setting, and no break in the flying vapour, and a blackness as of ink stealing into it out of the swift tropic dusk, I myself felt horribly dejected, greatly fearing that we had lost the brig for good.

Just before the last of the twilight faded out of the smoke that shrouded us, we lashed both oars together and, attaching them to the boat's painter, threw them overboard and rode to them. Our thirst was now extreme, and to appease it—being without a dipper to drop into the cask—we sank a handkerchief through the bung-hole and wrung it out in the half of a cocoa-nut shell that was in the boat as a baler, and by this means procured a drink, each man. Grateful to God indeed was I that we had fresh water with us. I beat the cask, and gathered by the sound that it was more

than half full.   Heaven was bounti-
ful too in providing us with biscuit.
It had been the luckiest of thoughts
on Jackson's part, though he had desired nothing more than to obtain a
relish for his own rations of buffalo
hump aboard.

I never remember the like of the
pitch darkness of that night.   There
was a moon, pretty nearly a full one
if I recollect aright ; but had she
been shining over the other side of
the world it would have been all the
same.   Her delicate silver beam could
not pierce the vapour, and never
once did I behold the least glistening
of her radiance anywhere.   There
was a constant noise of wind in the
dense thickness, and an incessant
seething and crackling of waters running nimbly, so that though we would
from time to time bend our ears in
the hope of catching the rushing and
pouring noise of the sea divided by
a ship's stem, we never could hear
more than the whistling of the breeze
and the lapping of the hurrying little
surges.   There was a deal of fire in
the water, and it came and went in
sheets like the reflection of lightning,
insomuch that we might have believed ourselves in the heart of an
electric storm ; but happily the wind
never gathered so much weight as to

raise a troublesome sea, and though the boat tumbled friskily she kept dry, and there was nothing in her movements to render me uneasy.

I told the two fellows to lie down in the bottom of the boat, and I kept watch till I reckoned it was drawing on to about one o'clock in the morning. Twice or thrice during that long and wretched vigil there seemed a promise of the weather clearing, and I gazed with the yearning of the shipwrecked ; but regularly it thickened and blackened down upon us again in blasts like the belchings of a three-decker's broadside. It was a very watery vapour, and I was early wet to the skin.

At about one o'clock, as I calculated, I awoke Jackson, and bade him keep an eager look-out and not to spare his ear in putting it against the night, "for," says I, "there 's nothing to be done with the eyes ; it 's all for the hearing at such a time as this, mate, and what you can't watch for you must listen for ; and wake me up to any sound you may hear, that our three throats may hail together. O God," says I, "if it would but thin and show the brig within reach of our shouts ! " With that I lay down and was soon fast asleep, being worn out with excitement and grief, and when I awoke it was daylight, for there's but little dawn off the Andamans; the sun in those seas leaps on to the horizon from the night as it were, and flashes it into day in a breath.

It was still thick and troubled weather, but clear to about two miles from the side of the boat. There was very little wind, and a long swell of the colour of lead was running from the southward. The vapour had broken up and lay in masses round about us—long, white twisted folds of it, like powder smoke after a great battle; and to the top of those heaps of thickness the sky sloped in a sort of grey shadow, with a little pencilling here and there of some small livid ring of mist, which looked stirless as though what air there was blew low. There was nothing in sight; we strained our gaze into every quarter but I saw there was nothing to be seen. This smote me to the heart. I had been in my time in several situations of peril at sea, but had never yet experienced the horrors of an open boat amidst a vast waste of waters, such as was this Bay of Bengal with the Andaman Islands some hundreds of miles distant, and a near menace of roasting heat when the wide grey stretch of cloud should have passed away and laid bare the sun's eye of fire. We gazed with melancholy faces one at another.

"What's to be done?" says Fallows, bringing his bloodshot eyes from the sea to my face; "if we had a sail to set we might have a chance."

"There are two oars," said I, "for a mast and a yard, and our shirts must furnish a sail."

"But how are we to head?" says Jackson.

"Right afore the wind, I suppose," says I; "there'll be no ratching with the rags we're going to hoist. Right afore the wind," I says; "and we must trust to God to keep us in view till something heaves in sight—which is pretty well bound to happen I suppose when there comes some wind along."

I opened the canvas parcel, and found a matter of thirty biscuits; all very sweet, good bread. We took each of us a piece, and followed on with a drink, and then went to work to get our oars in. We all three wore shirts, and we stripped them off our backs and cut them to lie open. I had a little circular cushion of stout pins in my pocket, such as a sailor might carry, and with them we brought the squares of the shirts to-

gether, and seized the corners to
one of the oars by yarns out of an
end of painter we cut off, then
stepped the other oar, and secured it
with another piece of the painter;
and now we had a sort of sail, the
mere sight of which, even, was a
small satisfaction to us, since the
shirts being white they must needs
make a good mark upon the water,
something not to be missed, unless
wilfully, by a passing vessel.

The morning passed away, and a
little after twelve o'clock the water
in the south was darkened by the
brushing of a wind, which drove the
hovering masses of vapour before it;
and presently they had totally disappeared, leaving a sky with rents and
yawns of blue in places, and a clear
glass-like circle of horizon, upon
which, however, there was nothing
to be seen. The boat moved slowly
before the wind, which blew hot as a
desert breeze; I steered, and Jackson and Fallows sat near me, one or
the other from time to time getting
on to a thwart to take a view of the
ocean, under the sharp of his hand.

In this fashion passed the afternoon. The night came with a deal
of fire in the water, and a very clear
moon floating in lagoons of velvet
softness betwixt the clouds. The

weather continued quiet ; the long
swell made a pleasant cradle of the
boat, and the night-wind being full
of dew, breathed refreshingly upon
our hot cheeks ; whilst our ears were
soothed by the rippling noise of the
running waters which seemed to cool
the senses, as the breeze did the
body.

It was almost a dead calm, however, at daybreak next morning.
The atmosphere was close and heavy,
and there was a strange strong smell
of seaweed, rising off the ocean,
which caused me to look narrowly
about, with some dim dream of per-
ceiving land, though I should have
known there was no land for leagues
and leagues.

Whilst we were munching a biscuit,
I observed an appearance of steam
lifting off the water, at a distance of
about half-a-mile on the starboard
side of the boat. The vapour came
out of the water in the shape of cork-
screws, spirally working, and they
melted at a height of perhaps ten or
fifteen feet. I counted five of these
singular emissions. Jackson said
that they were fragments of mist, and
we might look out for such another
thickness as had lost us the brig.
Fallows said : "No ; that's no mist,
mate ; that is as good steam as ever

blew out of a kettle. Are there places
where the water boils in this here
ocean ?"

As he said these words, an extraordinary thrill passed through the
boat, followed by a sound that
seemed more like an intellectual sensation than a real noise. What to
compare it to I don't know ; it was as
though it had thundered under the
sea. An instant later, up from the
part of the water where the corkscrew
appearances were, rose a prodigious
body of steam. It soared without a
sound from the deep ; it was balloon-
shaped but of mountainous proportions.

"A sea-quake !" roared Jackson.
"Stand by for the rollers !"

But no sea followed. I could witness no commotion whatever in the
water ; the light, long swell flowed
placidly into the base of the mass of
whiteness, and there was nothing besides visible on the breast of the sea,
save the delicate wrinkling of the
weak draught of air. Very quickly the
vapour thinned as steam does, and as
it melted off the surface, it disclosed
to our astonished gaze what at first
sight seemed to me the fabric of a
great ship, but after viewing it for a
moment or two, I distinctly made out
the form of an old-fashioned hull

with the half of much such another
hull as she, alongside, both apparently
locked together about the bows ;
and they seemed to be supported by
some huge gleaming black platform ;
but what it was we could not tell.

The three of us drew a deep breath
as we surveyed the floating objects.
The steam was gone ; there they lay
plain and bare ; it was as though the
wand of a magician had touched the
white mass and transformed it into
the objects we gazed at.

"Down with the sail," says I,
"there 's something yonder worth
looking at."

We got the oars over, and pulled in
the direction of the fabrics. As we
approached I could scarce credit the
evidence of my own sight. The form
of one of the vessels was perfect.
She was of an antique build, and belonged to a period that I reckoned
was full eighty years dead and gone.
The other—the half of her I should
say--showed a much bluffer bow, and
had been a vessel of some burthen.
But the wonder was the object on
which they rested This was no more
nor less than the body of a great dead
whale !

We first needed to lose something
of our amazement ere we could
reasonably speculate upon what we

saw ; then how this had happened grew plain to our minds. The two craft, God knows how many long years before, had been in action and foundered in conflict. The smaller vessel—I mean the one that lay whole before us—might have been a privateersman ; she had something of a piratical sheer forward, there were no signs of a mast aboard either of them, one had grappled the other to board her I dare say, and they had both gone to the bottom linked. The vessel of which only half remained may have broken her back in settling, and, by-and-bye, the after part of her drifted away, leaving the dead bows still gripped by the dead enemy alongside. But how came the whale there ? Well, we three men reasoned it thus, and I don't doubt we were right. At the moment of the sea-quake the whale was stemming steadily towards the two wrecks resting on the bottom. They were lifted by the explosion, which at the same time killed the whale ; but the impetus of the vast form slided it to under the lifted keels, where it came to a stand. A dead whale floats, as we know. This whale being dead was bound to rise, and the buoyancy of the immense mass brought the two craft up with it, and there they were.

poised by the gleaming surface of the whale, which was depressed by their weight, so that no portion of the head, tail, or fluke was visible.

"It's them vessels being connected," says Jackson, "as keeps them afloat. If what holds them together forrard was to part they 'd slide off that there slipperiness and sink."

We rowed close, the three of us greatly marvelling, as you may suppose, for never had the like of such an incident as this happened at sea within the knowledge of ever a one of us, and Fallows alone was a man of five and forty, who had been using the ocean for thirty-three years. It was as scaring as the rising of a corpse out of the depths—as scaring as if that corpse turned to and spoke when his head showed,—to see those two vessels lying in the daylight after eighty, aye, and perhaps a hundred years of the green silence hundreds of fathoms deep, locked in the same posture in which they had gone down, making you almost fancy that you could hear the thunder of their guns, witness the flashing of cutlasses, and the rush of the boarders to the bulwarks amidst a hurricane note of huzzaing and shrieks of the wounded.

They were both of them hand-

somely crusted with shells, not of the
barnacle sort, but such as you would
pick up anywhere in Ceylon or the
Andaman, some of them finely col-
oured, many of them white as milk,
of a thousand different patterns ; and
there was not one of them but what
was beautiful.

" Let 's board her," says Jackson.

" Ah, but if that whale be alive ! "
says Fallows.

" No fear of that," said I ; " if he
was alive there 'd be some stir in him.
The whale 's not the danger ; it 's the
lashing, which may part at any moment.   It should be in a fair way of
rottenness after so many years of salt
water, and if it goes the vessels go."

" I 'm for boarding her all the
same," says Jackson.

But first of all we pulled round to betwixt the bows of the craft to see what
it was that connected them, and we
found that they were held together
by something stronger than an old
grapnel.   The bluff of the bows came
together like walls cemented by sand
and shell, and it was easy by a mere
glance to perceive that they would
hold together whilst the sea continued tranquil.   Betwixt their heels
was a hollow which the round of the
whale nicely filled, and there they
all three lay, very slowly and sol-

9

emnly rolling upon the swell in as
deep a silence as ever they had risen
from.

We hung upon our oars speculating
awhile, and then fell to talking ourselves into extravagant notions. Fallows said that if she had been a
privateer she might have money in
her, or some purchase anyway worth
coming at. I was not for ridiculing
the fancy, and Jackson gazed at the
craft with a yearning eye.

"Let 's get aboard," says he.

"Very well," says I, and we agreed
that Fallows should keep in the boat
ready to pick us up, if the hulk should
go down suddenly under us. We
easily got aboard. From the gunwale of our boat we could place our
hands upon the level of the deck,
where the bulwarks were gone, and
the shells were like steps to our feet.
There was nothing much to be seen,
however; the decks were coated with
shells as the sides were, and they
went flush from the taffrail to the eyes
with never a break, everything being
clean gone, saving the line of the
hatches which showed in slightly
raised squares, under the crust of
shells that lay everywhere like
armour.

"Lord!" cried Jackson; "what
would I give for a chopper or pick-

axe to smash open that there hatch, so as to get inside of her."

" Inside of her ? " says I ; " why she 'll be full of water ! "

" That 's to be proved, Mr. Small," says he.

We walked forward into the bows, and clearly made out the shape of a grapnel thick with shells, with its claws upon the bulwark rail of the half-ship alongside, and there was a line stretched between, belayed to what might have been a kevel on a stanchion of the craft we were in. This rope was as lovely as a piece of fancy work, with tiny shells ; but on my touching it, to see if it was taut, it parted as if it had been formed of smoke, and each end fell with a little rattle against the side as though it had been a child's string of beads.

We were gaping about us, almost forgetting our distressed situation, in contemplation of these astonishing objects which had risen like ghosts from the mysterious heart of the deep, when we heard Fallows calling, and on our running to the side to learn what he wanted, we saw him standing up in the boat, pointing like a madman into the southward. It was the white canvas of a vessel, clearer to us than to him, who was lower by some feet. The air was still a weak draught, but the sail was rising with a nimbleness that made us know she was bringing a breeze of wind along with her, and in half-an-hour's time she had risen to the black line of her bulwarks rail, disclosing the fabric of what was apparently a brig or barque, heading almost dead on her end for us.

Jackson and I at once tumbled into the boat, but we were careful to keep her close to the two craft, and the amazing platform they floated on, for they furnished out a show that was not to be missed aboard the approaching vessel, whereas the boat must make little more than a speck though but half-a-mile distant.

The breeze the vessel was bringing along with her was all about us presently with a threat of weight in it. We stepped an oar, with the shirts atop, and they blew out bravely and made a good signal.

" Why, see, Mr. Small ! " cries Jackson, on a sudden, " ain't she the *Hindoo Merchant* ? "

I stood awhile, and then joyfully exclaimed, " Ay, 't is the old hooker herself, thanks be to God ! "

I knew her by her short fore-topgallantmast, by her chequered band, and by other signs clear to a sailor's eye, and the three of us sent up a shout of delight, for it was like stumbling upon one's very home, as it were, after having been all night lost amidst the blackness and snow of the country where one's house stands.

She came along handsomely, with foam to the hawsepipe, thanks to the freshening breeze, and her main royal and topgallantsail clewing up as she approached, for our signal had been seen ; then drove close alongside with her topsail aback and in a few minutes we were aboard, shaking hands with Captain Blow, and all others who extended a fist to us, and spinning our yarn in response to the eager questions put.

"But what have you there, Mr. Small?" said Captain Blow, staring at the two craft and the whale. I explained. "Well," cries he, "call me a missionary if ever I saw such a sight as that afore ! Have ye boarded the vessel ?" pointing to the one that was whole.

"Yes," said I, "but there's nothing but shells to look at."

"Hatches open ?" says he.

"No," says I, "they are as securely cemented with shells as if the stuff had been laid on with a trowel."

Jackson, Fallows, the boatswain, and a few of the darkeys stood near, eagerly catching what we said.

"A wonderful sight truly!" said Captain Blow, surveying the object with a face almost distorted with astonishment and admiration. "How many years will they have been asleep under water, think ye, Mr. Small?"

"All a hundred, sir," said I.

"Ay," says he, "I've seen many prints of old ships, and I'll allow that it's all a hundred, as you say, since she and the likes of she was afloat. Why," cries he with a sort of a nervous laugh as if half ashamed of what he was about to say, "who's to tell but that there may be a chest or two of treasure stowed away down in her lazerette?"

"That very idea occurred to me, sir," says I.

"By your pardon, capt'n," here interrupted Jackson, knuckling his forehead, "but that may be a question not hard to settle if ye'll send me aboard with a few tools."

The captain looked as if he had had a mind to entertain the idea, then sent a glance to windward.

"She'll be full of water," said I.

"Ay," said the captain, turning to Jackson, "how then?"

"We can but lift a hatch and look out for ourselves, sir," answered the man.

"Right," says the captain; "but

you 'll have to bear a hand. Get
that cask on board. Any water in
it ?" says he.

"Yes, sir," says I.

" Thank God for the same then,"
says he.

But whilst they were manœuvring
with the cask the breeze freshened in
a sudden squall, and all in a minute,
as it seemed, a sort of sloppy sea was
set a-running. The captain looked
anxious, yet still seemed willing that
the boat should go to the wreck. I
sent some Lascars aloft to furl the
loose canvas, and whilst this was
doing, the wind freshened yet in
another long-drawn blast that swept
in a shriek betwixt our masts.

" There 's nothing to be done ! "
sung out the skipper ; " get that boat
under the fall, Jackson ; we must
hoist her up."

The darkeys lay aft to the tackles,
and Jackson climbed over the rail
with a countenance sour and muti-
nous with disappointment. He had
scarcely sprung on to the deck, when
we heard a loud crash like the report
of a small piece of ordnance, and,
looking towards the hulks, I was just
in time to see them sliding off the
back of the whale, one on either side
of the greasy, black surface. They
vanished in a breath, and the dead

carcass, relieved of their weight, seemed to spring, as though it were alive, some ten or twelve feet out of the seething and simmering surface which had been frothed up by the descent of the vessels ; the next moment it turned over and gave us a view of its whole length—a sixty- to seventy-foot whale, if the carcass was an inch, with here and there the black scythe-like dorsal fin of a shark sailing round it.

Jackson hooked a quid out of his mouth and sent it overboard. His face of mutiny left him, and was replaced by an expression of gratitude. Five minutes later the old *Hindoo Merchant* was thrusting through it with her nose heading for the river Hooghley, and the darkeys tying a single reef in the foretopsail.

The Strange Tragedy of the " White Star."

IT is proper I should state at once that the names I give in this extraordinary experience are fictitious; the date of the tale is easily within the memory of the middle-aged.

The large, well-known Australian liner *White Star* lay off the wool-sheds in Sydney harbour slowly filling up with wool; I say slowly, for the oxen were languid up-country, and the stuff came in as Fox is said to have written his history—" drop by drop." We were, however, advertised to sail in a fortnight from the day I open this story on, and there was no doubt of our getting away by then.

I, who was chief officer of the vessel, was pacing the poop under the awning, when I saw a lady and gentleman approaching the vessel. They spoke to the mate of a French barque which lay just ahead of us, and I

concluded that their business was
with that ship, till I saw the French-
man, with a flourish of his hat, motion
towards the *White Star*, whereupon
they advanced and stepped on board.

I went on to the quarter-deck to
receive them. The gentleman had
the air of a military man : short,
erect as a royal mast, with plenty of
whiskers and moustache, though he
wore his chin cropped. His companion was a very fine young woman
of about six and twenty years ; above
the average height, faultlessly shaped,
so far as a rude seafaring eye is
privileged to judge of such matters;
her complexion was pale, inclined to
sallow, but most delicate, of a trans-
parency of flesh that showed the
blood eloquent in her cheek, coming
and going with every mood that possessed her. She wore a little fall of
veil, but she raised it when her companion handed her over the side in
order to look round and aloft at the
fabric of spar and shroud towering
on high, with its central bunting of
house flag pulling in ripples of gold
and blue from the royalmast head ;
and so I had a good sight of her face,
and particularly of her eyes.

I never remember the like of such
eyes in a woman. To describe them
as neither large nor small, the pupils

of the liquid dusk of the Indian's, the
eyelashes long enough to cast a silken
shadow of tenderness upon the whole
expression of her face when the lids
dropped—to say all this is to convey
nothing ; simply because their expression formed the wonder, strange-
ness, and beauty of them, and there
is no virtue in ink, at all events in
my ink, to communicate it.   I do not
exaggerate when I assure you that
the surprise of the beauty of her eyes
when they came to mine and rested
upon me, steadfast in their stare as a
picture, was a sort of shock in its
way, comparable in a physical sense
to one's unexpected handling of
something slightly electric.   For the
rest, her hair was very black and
abundant, and of that sort of dead-
ness of hue which you find among the
people of Asia.   I cannot describe
her dress.   Enough if I say that she
was in mourning, but with a large
admixture of white, for those were
the hot weeks in Sydney.

"Is the captain on board ? " in-
quired the gentleman.

" He is not, sir."

"When do you expect him ? "

" Every minute."

" May we stop here ? "

"Certainly.   Will you walk into
the cuddy or on to the poop ? "

"Oh, we'll keep in the open, we'll keep in the open," cried the gentleman, with the impetuosity of a man rendered irritable by the heat. "You'll have had enough of the cuddy, Miss Le Grand, long before you reach the old country."

She smiled. I liked her face then. It was a fine, glad, good-humoured smile, and humanised her wonderful eyes just as though you clothed a ghost in flesh, making the spectre natural and commonplace.

As we ascended the poop ladder, the gentleman asked me who I was, quite courteously, though his whole manner was marked by a quality of military abruptness. When he understood I was chief officer he exclaimed :

"Then Miss Le Grand permit me to introduce Mr. Tyler to you. Miss Georgina Le Grand is going home in your ship. She will be alone. We have placed her in the care of the captain."

"Perhaps," said Miss Le Grand with another of her fine smiles, " I ought to introduce you, Mr. Tyler, to my uncle, Colonel Atkinson.

Again I pulled off my cap, and the colonel laughed as he lifted his wide straw hat. I guessed he laughed at a

certain naïvete in the girl's way of
introducing us.

The colonel was disposed to chat.
Out of England Englishmen are
amongst the most talkative of the
human race. Likely enough he
wanted to interest me in Miss Le
Grand because of my situation on
board. A chief mate is a considerable
figure. If any mishap incapacitates
the master, the chief mate takes
charge. We walked the poop, the
three of us, in the violet shadow cast
by the awning; the colonel constantly
directed his eyes along the quay to
observe if the captain was coming.
During this stroll to and fro the white
planks I got these particulars, partly
from the direct assertions of the
colonel, partly from the occasional
remarks of the girl.

Colonel Atkinson had married her
father's sister. Her father had been
an officer in the army, and had sailed
from England with the then Governor
of New South Wales. After he had
been in Sydney a few months he sent
for his daughter, whom he had left
behind him with a maternal aunt, her
mother having died some years before. She reached Sydney to find
her father dead. His Excellency was
very kind to her, and she found very

many sympathetic friends, but her
home was in England, and to it she
was returning in the *White Star*,
under the care of the master, Captain
Edward Griffiths, after a stay of nearly
five months in Sydney with her uncle,
Colonel Atkinson.

Half an hour passed before the
captain arrived. When he stepped
on board I lifted my cap and left the
poop, and the captain and the others
went into the cuddy.

Our day of departure came round,
and not a little rejoiced was I when
the tug had fairly got hold of us, and
we were floating over the sheet-calm
surface of Sydney Bay, past some of
the loveliest bits of scenery the world
has to offer, on our road to the
mighty ocean beyond the grim portals
of Sydney Heads. We were a fairly
crowded ship, what with Jacks and
passengers. The steerage and 'tween-
decks were full up with people going
home; in the cuddy some of the
cabins remained unlet. We mustered
in all, I think, about twelve gentlemen
and lady passengers, one of whom,
needless to say, was Miss Georgina
Le Grand.

I had been busy on the forecastle
when she came aboard, but heard
afterwards from Robson, the second
mate, that the Governor's wife, with

Colonel Atkinson, and certain nobs
out of Government House had driven
down to the ship to say good-bye to
the girl. She was alone. I wondered
she had not a maid, but I afterwards
heard from a bright little lady on board,
a Mrs. Burney, one of the wickedest
flirts that ever with a flash of dark
glance drew a sigh from a man, that
the woman Miss Le Grand had engaged to accompany her as maid to
Europe had omitted to put in an
appearance at the last moment, in
perfect conformity with the manners
and habits of the domestic servants
of the Australian colonies of those
days, and the young lady having no
time to procure another maid had
shipped alone.

At dinner on that first day of our
departure, when the ship was at sea
and I was stumping the deck in
charge, I observed, in glancing
through the skylight, that the captain
had put Miss Le Grand upon the
right of his chair, at the head of the
table, a little before the fluted and
emblazoned shaft of mizzenmast. I
don't think above five sat down to
dinner; a long heave of swell had
sickened the hunger out of most of
them. But it was a glorious evening,
and the red sunshine, flashing fair
upon the wide open skylights, dazzled

out as brilliant and hospitable a picture of cabin equipment as the sight
could wish.

I had a full view of Miss Le Grand,
and occasionally paused to look at
her, so standing as to be unobserved.
Now that I saw her with her hat off I
found something very peculiar and
fascinating in her beauty. Her eyes
seemed to fill her face, subduing
every lineament to the full spiritual
light and meaning in them, till her
countenance looked sheer intellect,
the very quality and spirit of mind
itself. This effect, I think, was largely
achieved by the uncommon hue of
her skin. It accentuated colour, casting a deeper dye into the blackness
of her hair, sharpening the fires in
her eyes, painting her lips with a
more fiery tinge of carnation through
which, when she smiled, her white
teeth shone like light itself.

I noticed even on this first day,
during my cautious occasional peeps,
that the captain was particularly at-
tentive to the young lady ; in which,
indeed, I should have found nothing
significant—for she had in a special
degree been committed to his trust—
but for the circumstance of his being
a bachelor. Even then, early and
fresh as the time was for thinking of
such things, I guessed when I looked

at the girl that the hardy mariner
alongside of her would not keep his
heart whole a week, if indeed, for the
matter of that, he was not already
head over ears. He was a good-look-
ing man in his way ; not everybody's
type of manly beauty, perhaps, but
certain of admiration from those who
relish a strong sea flavour and the
colour of many years and countless
leagues of ocean in looks, speech, and
deportment. He was about thirty-
five, the heartiest laugher that ever
strained a rib in merriment, a genial,
kindly man, with a keen, seawardly
blue eye, weather-coloured face, short
whiskers, and rising in his socks to
near six feet. I believe he was of
Welsh blood. This was my first
voyage with him. The rigorous discipline of the quarter-deck had held
us apart, and all that I could have
told of him I have here written.

For some time after we left Sydney
nothing whatever noteworthy happened. One quiet evening I came
on deck at eight o'clock to take
charge of the ship till midnight. We
were still in the temperate parallels,
the weather of a true Pacific sweet-
ness, and, by day, the ocean a dark
blue rolling breast of water, feather-
ing on every round of swell in sea-
flashes, out of which would sparkle

10

the flying-fish to sail down the bright mild wind for a space, then vanish in some brow of brine with the flight of a silver arrow.

This night the moon was dark, the weather somewhat thick, the stars pale over the trucks, and hidden in the obscurity a little way down the dusky slope of firmament. Windsails were wriggling fore and aft like huge white snakes, gaping for the tops and writhing out of the hatches. The flush of sunset was dying when I came on deck. I saw the captain slowly pacing the weather side of the poop with Miss Le Grand. He seemed earnest in his talk and gestures. Enough western light still lived to enable me to see faces, and I observed that Mrs. Burney, standing to leeward of a skylight talking with a gentleman, would glance at the couple with a satirical smile whenever they came abreast of her.

But soon the night came down in darkness upon the deep; the wind blew damp out of the dusk in a long moan over the rail, heeling the ship yet by a couple of degrees; the captain sang out for the fore- and mizzen-royals to be clewed up and furled, and shortly afterwards went below, first handing Miss Le Grand down the companion-way.

I guessed the game was up with
the worthy man : he had met his fate
and taken to it with the meekness of
a sheep. He might do worse, I
thought, as I started on a solitary
stroll, so far as looks are concerned ;
but what of her nature—her character ? It was puzzling to think of
what sort of spirit it was that looked
out of her wonderful eyes ; and she
was not a kind of a girl that a man
would care to leave ashore ; so much
beauty, full of a subtle endevilment of
some sort, as it seemed to me, must
needs demand the constant sentinel-
ling of a husband's presence. That
was how it struck me.

By eleven o'clock all was hushed
throughout the ship : lights out, the
captain turned in, nothing stirring
forward save the flitting shape of the
look-out under the yawn of the pale
square of fore-course. It was blowing a pleasant breeze of wind, and
lost in thought I leaned over the rail
at the weather fore-end of the poop
watching the cold sea-glow shining in
the dark water as the foam spat past,
sheeting away astern in a furrow like
moonlight. I will swear I did not
doze ; that I never was guilty of
whilst on duty in all the years I was
at sea ; but I don't doubt that I was
sunk deep in thought, insomuch that

my reverie may have possessed a
temporary power of abstraction as
complete as slumber itself.

I was startled into violent wakeful-
ness by a cannonade of canvas aloft,
and found the ship in the wind. I
looked aft ; the wheel was deserted
—at least I believed so, till on rushing to it, meanwhile shouting to the
watch on deck, I spied the figure of
the helmsman on his face close beside
the binnacle.

I thought he was dead. The watch
to my shouts came tumbling to the
braces, and in a few minutes the captain made his appearance. The ship
was got to her course afresh, by which
time the man who had been steering
was so far recovered as to be able to
sit on the grating abaft the wheel and
relate what had happened.

He was a Dane, and spoke with a
strong foreign accent, beyond my art
to reproduce. He said he had been
looking away to leeward, believing he
saw a light out upon the horizon,
when on turning his head he beheld
a ghost at his side.

" A what ? " said the captain.

" A ghost, sir, so help me—" and
here the little Dane indulged in some
very violent language, all designed to
convince us that he spoke the truth.

"What was it like?" asked the captain.

"It was dressed in white and stood looking at me. I tried to run and could not, but fell, and maybe fainted."

"The durned idiot slept," said the captain to me, "and dreamt, and dropped on his nut."

"Had I dropped on my nut, should not have woke up then?" cried the Dane, in a passion of candour.

"Go forward and turn in," said the captain. "The doctor shall see you and report to me."

When the man was gone the captain asked me if I had seen anything likely to produce the impression of a ghost on an ignorant, credulous man's mind? I answered no, wondering that he should ask such a question.

"How long was the man in a fit, d'ye think?" said he, "that is, before you found out that the wheel was deserted?"

"Three or four minutes."

He looked into the binnacle, took a turn about the decks, and, without saying anything more about the ghost, went below.

The doctor next day reported that the Dane was perfectly well, and of sound mind, and that he stuck with

many imprecations to his story. He
described the ghost as a figure in
white that looked at him with spark-
ling eyes, and yet blindly. He was
unable to describe the features.
Fright, no doubt, stood in the way of
perception. He could not imagine
where the thing had come from. He
was, as he had said, gazing at what
looked like a spark or star to leeward,
when turning his head he found the
Shape close beside him.

The captain and the doctor talked
the thing over in my presence, and
we decided to consider it a delusion
on the part of the Dane, a phantom
of his imagination, mainly because
the man swooned after he saw the
thing, letting go the wheel so that
the ship came up into the wind,
and it was impossible to conceive
that a substantial object could have
vanished in the time that elapsed between the man falling down and the
flap of sails which had called my attention to the abandoned helm.

However, nothing was said about
the matter aft : the sailors adopted
the doctor's opinion, some viewing
the thing as a " Dutchman's " dodge
to get a " night in."

A few days later brought us into
cold weather : this was followed by
the ice and conflicts of the Horn.

We drove too far south, and for a
week every afternoon we hove-to
under a close-reefed maintopsail for
fear of the ice throughout the long
hours of Antarctic blackness. We
were in no temper to think of ghosts,
and yet though no one had delivered
the news authoritatively, it had come
by this wild bleak time to be known
that Captain Griffiths and Miss Le
Grand were engaged. Mrs. Burney
told me so one day in the cuddy,
and with a wicked flash of her dark
eye wondered that people could think
of making love with icebergs close at
hand.

It was no business of mine, and
seemingly I gave the matter no heed,
though I could find leisure and curiosity sometimes for an askant glance
at the captain and his beauty when
they were at table or when the weather permitted the lady to come on
deck, and their behaviour left me in
very little doubt that he was deeply
in love with her; but whether she
was equally enamoured of him I
could not guess.

We beat clear of the latitude of
roaring gales blind with snow, and
mountainous ice-islands like cities of
alabaster in ruins, and seas ridging in
thunder and foam to the height of
our mizzentop, and heading north

blew under wide wings of studding
sails towards the sun, every day sinking some southern stars out of sight,
and every night lifting above the sea-
line some gem of the heavens dear to
northern eyes.

I went below at eight bells on a
Friday morning when we were two
months "out" from Sydney, as I
very well remember. The ship had
then caught the first of the south-east
trade-wind. All was well when I left
the deck. I was awakened by a hand
violently shaking my shoulder. I
sprang up and found Robson, the
second mate, standing beside my
bunk. He was pale as the ghost the
Dane had described.

"There 's been murder done, sir,"
he cried. "The captain 's killed."

I stared at him like a fool, and
echoed mechanically and dully:
"Murder done! Captain killed!"
Then collecting my wits I tumbled
into my clothes and rushed to the
captain's cabin, where I found the
doctor and the third mate examining
poor Griffith's body. It was half-
past-six o'clock in the morning, and
the daylight strong, but none of the
passengers were moving. The captain had been stabbed to the heart.
The doctor said he had been killed
by a single thrust. The body was

clothed in white drill trousers and a
white linen shirt, which was slightly
stained with blood where the knife
had pierced it.

Who had done this thing? It
was horrible, unprovoked murder!
throughout the ship the captain had
been the most popular man on
board. The forecastle liking for him
was as strong as sentiment of any
sort can find expression in that part
of a vessel. There had never been a
murmur. Indeed I had never sailed
with a better crew. Not a man had
deserted us at Sydney and of the
hands on board at least half had
sailed with the captain before.

We carefully searched the cabin, but
there was nothing whatever to tell us
that robbery had been committed.
However, a ghastly, shocking murder
had been perpetrated ; the man on
whose skill and judgment had de-
pended the safety of the ship and the
many lives within her had been foully
done to death in his sleep by some
mysterious hand, and we determined
at once upon a course.

First, I sent for some of the best and
most trustworthy seamen amongst
the crew, and bringing them into the
captain's cabin, showed them the
body. I then, in my capacity as
commander of the vessel, authorised

them to act as a sort of detectives or
policemen, and to search every part
of the ship and all the berths in the
steerage and 'tween-decks for any
clue to the doer of the deed. It was
arranged that the cabins of the first-
class passengers should be thoroughly
overhauled by the second and third
mates.

All this brought us to the hour
when the passengers arose, and the
ship was presently alive. The news
swept from lip to lip magically ; in all
parts of the ship I saw men and
women talking, with their faces pale
with consternation and horror. I
had not the courage to break the
news to Miss Le Grand, and asked
the doctor, a quiet, gentlemanly man,
to speak to her. I was on the poop
looking after the ship when the
doctor came from the young lady's
berth.

" How did she receive the news ? "
said I.

" I wish it may not break her
heart," said he, gravely. " She was
turned into stone. Her stare of
grief was dreadful—not the greatest
actress could imagine such a look.
There 'll be no comforting her this
side of England."

" Doctor, could he have done it
himself ? "

" Oh, heaven, no, sir ! " and he explained, by recalling the posture of
the body and the situation of the
hands, not to mention the absence of
the weapon, why it was impossible
the captain should have killed himself.

I don't know how it came about ;
but whilst I paced the deck waiting
for the reports of the mates and the
seamen and the passengers who were
helping me in the search, it entered
my head to mix up with this murder
the spectre, or ghost, that had frightened the Dane at the wheel into a fit,
along with the memory of a sort of
quarrel which I guessed had happened between Captain Griffiths and
Miss Le Grand. It was a mere mud-
dle of fancies at best, and yet they
took a hold of my imagination. I
think it was about a week before
this murder that I had observed the
coolness of what you might call a
lovers' quarrel betwixt the captain
and his young lady, and without taking any further notice of it I quietly
set the cause down to Mrs. Burney,
who, as a thorough-paced flirt, with
fine languishing black eyes, and a
saucy tongue, had often done her
best to engage the skipper in one of
those little asides which are as brim-
stone and the undying worm to the

jealous of either sex. The lovers had made it up soon after, and for two or three days previously had been as thick and lover-like as sweethearts ought to be.

But what had the ghost that had affrighted the Dane to do with this murder? And how were Mrs. Burney's blandishments, and the short-lived quarrel betwixt the lovers to be associated with it? Nevertheless, these matters ran in my head as I walked the deck on the morning of that crime, and I thought and thought, scarce knowing, however, in what direction imagination was heading.

The two mates, the seamen, and the passengers arrived with their reports. They had nothing to tell. The steward and the stewardess had searched with the two mates in the saloon or cuddy. Every cabin had been ransacked, with the willing consent of its occupants. The forecastle, and 'tween-decks, and steerage, and lazarette had been minutely overhauled. Every accessible part of the bowels of the ship had been visited ; to no purpose. No stowaway of any sort, no rag of evidence, or weapon to supply a clue was discovered.

That afternoon we buried the body and I took command of the ship.

I saw nothing of Miss Le Grand

for two days. She kept her cabin, and was seen only by the stewardess, who waited upon her. At the expiration of that time I received a message, and went at once to her berth. I never could have figured so striking a change in a fine woman full of beauty in so short a time, as I now beheld. The fire had died out of her eyes, and still there lurked something weird in the very spiritlessness, and dull and vacant sadness of her gaze. Her cheeks were hollow. Under each eye rested a shadow as though it was cast by a green leaf.

Her first words were : "Cannot you find out who did it?"

" No, madam. We have tried hard ; harder for the captain's sake than had he been another, for the responsibility that rests upon the master of an ocean-going vessel makes him an object of mighty significance, believe me, to us sailors."

" But the person who killed him must be in the ship," she cried, in a voice that wanted much of its old clear music.

"One should suppose so ; and he is undoubtedly on board the ship ; but we can't find him."

" Did he commit suicide?"

" No. Everybody is accounted for."

" What motive," she exclaimed, with a sudden burst of desperate passionate grief, that wrung her like a fit from head to foot, " could any one have for killing Captain Griffiths? He was the gentlest, the kindest—oh, my heart ! my heart !" and, hiding her face, she rocked herself in her misery.

I tried my rough, seafaring best to soothe her. Certainly, until this moment I never could have supposed her love for the poor man was so great.

The fear bred of this mysterious assassination lay in a dark and heavy shadow upon the ship. None of us, passengers or sailors, turned in of a night but with a fear of the secret bloody hand that had slain the captain making its presence tragically known once more before the morning.

It happened one midnight, when we were something north of the equator, in the calms and stinging heat of the inter-tropic latitudes, that, having come on deck to relieve the second mate, and take charge of the ship till four o'clock, I felt thirsty, and returned to the cuddy for a drink of water. Of the three lamps only one was alight, and burnt very dimly. There was no moonlight, but a plenty of starshine, which showered in a very rippling of spangled silver through

the yawning casements of the skylights.

Just as I returned the tumbler to
the rack whence I had removed it,
the door of Miss Le Grand's cabin
was opened, and the girl stepped
forth. She was arrayed in white;
probably she was attired in her bed-
clothes. She seemed to see me at
once, for she emerged directly oppo-
site; and I thought she would speak,
or hastily retire. But, after appear-
ing to stare for a little while, she
came to the table and leaned upon it
with her left hand, sighing several
times in the most heart-broken manner; and now I saw by the help of
the dim lamp light that her right hand
grasped a knife—the gleam of the
blade caught my eye in a breath!

"Good gracious!" I cried to myself, instantly, "the woman 's asleep!
This, then, is the ghost that frightened the Dane. And this, too, was
the hand that murdered the captain!"

I stood motionless watching her.
Presently, taking her hand off the
table, she turned her face aft, and
with a wonderfully subtle, stealthy,
sneaking gait, reminding one strangely
of the folding motion of the snake,
she made for the captain's cabin.

Now, that cabin, ever since Grif-

fith's death, I had occupied, and you
may guess the sensations with which
I followed the armed and murderous
sleep-walker as she glided to what I
must call my berth, and noiselessly
opened the door of it. The moment
she was in the cabin her motions
grew amazingly swift. She stepped
to the side of the bunk I was in the
habit of using, and lifting the knife
plunged it once, deep and hard—then
came away, so nimbly that it was with
difficulty I made room for her in the
doorway to pass. I heard her breathe
hard and fast as she swept by, and I
stood in the doorway of my cabin
watching her till her figure disappeared in her own berth.

So, then, the mystery was at an end.
Poor Captain Griffith's murderess was
his adored sweetheart! She had
killed him in her sleep, and knew it
not. In the blindness of slumber she
had repeated the enormous tragedy, as
sinless nevertheless as the angel who
looked down and beheld her and
pitied her!

I went on deck and sent for the
doctor, to whom I communicated
what I had seen, and he at once re-
paired to Miss Le Grand's berth accompanied by the stewardess, and
found her peacefully resting in her
bunk. No knife was to be seen.

However, next morning, the young lady being then on deck, veiled as she always now went, and sitting in a retired part of the poop, the second mate, the doctor, and the stewardess again thoroughly searched Miss Le Grand's berth, and they found in a hollow in the ship's side, a sort of scupper in fact for the porthole, a carving knife, rusted with old stains of blood. It had belonged to the ship, and it was a knife the steward had missed on the day the captain was killed.

Since the whole ghastly tragedy was a matter of somnambulism, all points of it were easily fitted by the doctor, who quickly understood that the knife had been taken by the poor girl in her sleep just as it had been murderously used. What horrible demon governed her in her slumber, who shall tell? For my part I put it down to Mrs. Burney and a secret feeling of jealousy which had operated in the poor soul when sense was suspended in her by slumber.

We tried to keep the thing secret, taking care to lock Miss Le Grand up every night without explaining our motive; but the passengers got wind of the truth and shrunk from her with horror. It came, in fact, to their waiting upon me in a body and

11

insisting upon my immuring her in the steerage in company with one of the 'tween-deck's passengers, a female who had offered her services as a nurse for hire. This action led to the poor girl herself finding out what had happened. God knows who told her or how she managed to discover it ; but 't is certain she got to learn it was her hand that in sleep had killed her lover, and she went mad the selfsame day of her understanding what she had done.

Nor did she ever recover her mind. She was landed mad, and sent at once to an asylum, where she died, God rest her poor soul ! exactly a year after the murder, passing away, in fact, at the very hour the deed was done, as I afterwards heard.

The Ship Seen on the Ice.

IN the middle of April, in the year 1855, the three-masted schooner *Lightning* sailed from the Mersey for Boston with a small general cargo of English manufactured goods. She was commanded by a man named Thomas Funnel. The mate, Salamon Sweers, was of Dutch extraction, and his broad-beamed face was as Dutch to the eye as was the sound of his name to the ear. Yet he spoke English with as good an accent as ever one could hear in the mouth of an Englishman; and, indeed, I pay Salamon Sweers no compliment by saying this, for he employed his *h's* correctly, and the grammar of his sentences was fairly good, albeit salt: and how many Englishmen are there who correctly employ the letter *h*, and whose grammar is fairly good, salt or no salt?

We carried four forecastle hands and three apprentices. There was

Charles Petersen, a Swede, who had once been "fancy man" in a toy shop; there was David Burton, who had been a hairdresser and proved unfortunate as a gold-digger in Australia; there was James Lussoni, an Italian, who claimed to be a descendant of the old Genoese merchants; and there was John Jones, a runaway man-of-warsman, pretty nearly worn out, and subject to apoplexy.

Four sailors and three apprentices make seven men, a cook and a boy are nine, and a mate and a captain make eleven; and eleven of a crew were we, all told, men and boy, aboard the three-masted schooner *Lightning* when we sailed away one April morning out of the river Mersey, bound to Boston, North America.

My name was then as it still is—for during the many years I have used the sea, never had I occasion to ship with a "purser's name"—my name, I say, is David Kerry, and in that year of God 1855 I was a strapping young fellow, seventeen years old, making a second voyage with Captain Funnel, having been bound apprentice to that most excellent but long-departed mariner by my parents, who, finding me resolved to go to sea had determined that my probation should be thorough: no half-

laughs and pursers' grins would
satisfy them ; my arm was to plunge
deep into the tar bucket straight
away ; and certainly there was no
man then hailing from the port of
Liverpool better able to qualify a
young chap for the profession of the
sea—but a young chap, mind you,
who liked his calling, who *meant* to
be a man and not a " sojer " in it—
than Captain Funnel of the schooner
Lightning.

The four sailors slept in a bit of a
forecastle forward ; we three apprentices slung our hammocks in a bulk-
headed part of the run or steerage,
a gloomy hole, the obscurity of which
was defined rather than illuminated
by the dim twilight sifting down
aslant from the hatch. Here we
stowed our chests, and here we took
our meals, and here we slept and
smoked and yarned in our watch below. I very well remember my two
fellow apprentices. One was named
Corbin, and the other Halsted. They
were both of them smart, honest,
bright lads, coming well equipped
and well educated from respectable
homes, in love with the calling of the
sea, and resolved in time not only to
command ships, but to own them.

Well, nothing in any way noteworthy happened for many days.

Though the schooner was called the *Lightning*, she was by no means a clipper. She was built on lines which were fashionable forty years before, when the shipwright held that a ship's stability must be risked if she was one inch longer than five times her beam. She was an old vessel, but dry as a stale cheese; wallowed rather than rolled, yet was stiff; would sit upright with erect spars, like the cocked ears of a horse, in breezes which bowed passing vessels down to their wash-streaks. Her round bows bruised the sea, and when it entered her head to take to her heels, she would wash through it like a "gallied whale," all smothered to the hawse-pipes, and a big round polished hump of brine on either quarter.

We ambled, and wallowed, and blew, and in divers fashions drove along till we were deep in the heart of the North Atlantic. It was then a morning that brought the first of May within a biscuit-toss of our reckoning of time : a very cold morning, the sea flat, green, and greasy, with a streaking of white about it, as though it were a flooring of marble ; there was wind but no lift in the water ; and Salamon Sweers, in whose watch I was, said to me, when the day broke and showed us the look of the ocean :

"Blowed," said he, "if a man might n't swear that we were under the lee of a range of high land."

It was very cold, the wind about north-west, the sky a pale grey, with patches of weak hazy blue in it here and there ; and here and there again lay some darker shadow of cloud curled clean as though painted. There was nothing in sight saving the topmost cloths of a little barque heading eastwards away down to lee-ward. Quiet as the morning was, not once during the passage had I found the temperature so cold. I was glad when the job of washing down was over, and not a little grate-ful for the hook-pot of steam tea which I took from the galley to my quarters in the steerage.

I breakfasted in true ocean fash-ion, off ship's biscuit, a piece of pork, the remains of yesterday's din-ner, and a potful of black liquor called tea, sweetened by molasses and thickened with sodden leaves and fragments of twigs ; and then, cutting a pipeful of tobacco from a stick of cavendish, I climbed into my hammock, and lay there smoking and trying to read in Norie's *Epitome* until my pipe went out, on which I fell asleep.

I was awakened by young Halsted, whose hand was upon the edge of my hammock.

"Not time to turn out yet, I hope?" I exclaimed. "I don't feel to have been below ten minutes."

"There's the finest sight to see on deck," said he, "that you're likely to turn up this side of Boston. Tumble up and have a look if only for five minutes"; and without another word he hastened up the ladder.

I dropped out of my hammock, pulled on my boots and monkey-jacket, and went on deck, noting the hour by the cabin clock to be twenty minutes before eleven. The captain stood at the mizzen-rigging with a telescope at his eye, and beside him stood Mr. Sweers, likewise holding a glass, and both men pointed their telescopes towards the sea on the lee bow, where—never having before beheld an iceberg—I perceived what I imagined to be an island covered with snow.

An iceberg it was—not a very large one. It was about five miles distant; it had a ragged sky line which made it resemble a piece of cliff gone adrift—such a fragment

of cliff as, let me say, a quarter of a
mile of the chalk of the South Fore-
land would make, if you can imagine a mass of the stuff detaching
itself from under the verdure at the
top and floating off jagged and pre-
cipitous. There was nothing to be
seen but that iceberg. No others.
The sea ran smooth as oil, and of a
hard green, piebald foam lines as in
the earlier morning, with but a light
swell out of the west, which came
lifting stealthily to the side of the
schooner. There was a small breeze ;
the sky had a somewhat gloomy
look ; the schooner was at this hour
crawling along at the rate of about
four and a half knots.

I said to Halsted : " There was
nothing in sight when I went below
at eight bells. Where 's that berg
come from ? "

" From behind the horizon," he
answered. " The breeze freshened
soon after you left the deck, and
only slackened a little while since."

" What can they see to keep them
staring so hard ? " said I, referring
to the captain and Mr. Sweers, who
kept their glasses steadily levelled at
the iceberg.

" They 've made out a ship upon
the ice," he answered ; " a ship high
and dry upon a slope of foreshore.

I believe I can see her now—the gleam of the snow is confusing; there's a black spot at the base almost amidships of the berg."

I had a good sight in those days. I peered awhile and made out the object, but with the naked eye I could never have distinguished it as a ship at that distance.

"She's a barque," I heard Mr. Sweers say.

"I see that," said the captain.

"She's got a pretty strong list," continued the mate, talking with the glass at his eye; "her topgallant-masts are struck, but her topmasts are standing."

"I tell you what it is," said the captain, after a pause, likewise speaking whilst he gazed through his telescope, "that ship's come down somewhere from out of the North Pole. She never could have struck the ice and gone ashore as we see her there. She's been locked up; then the piece she's on broke away and made sail to the south. I've fallen in with bergs with live polar bears on them in my time."

"What is she—a whaler?" said Mr. Sweers. "She's got a lumbersome look about the bulwarks, as though she wasn't short of cranes; but I can't make out any boats, and there 's no appearance of life aboard her."

" Let her go off a point," said the captain to the fellow at the wheel. " Mr. Sweers, she 'll be worth looking at," he continued, slowly directing his gaze round the sea-line, as though considering the weather. ' You 've heard of Sir John Franklin ? "

" Have I heard ?" said the mate, with a Dutch shrug.

"It 's the duty of every English sailor," said the captain, " to keep his weather eye lifting whenever he smells ice north of the equator ; for who 's to tell what relics of the Franklin expedition he may not light on ? And how are we to know," continued he, again directing his glass at the berg, " that yonder vessel may not have taken part in that expedition ? "

" There 's a reward going," said Mr. Sweers, " for the man who can discover anything about Sir John Franklin and his party."

The captain grinned and quickly grew grave.

We drew slowly towards the iceberg, at which I gazed with some degree of disappointment ; for, never before having beheld ice in a great mass like the heap that was yonder, I had expected to see something admirable and magnificent, an island of

glass, full of fiery sparklings and ruby
and emerald beams, a shape of crystal cut by the hand of King Frost
into a hundred inimitable devices.
Instead of which, the island of ice,
on which lay the hull of the ship,
was of a dead, unpolished whiteness,
abrupt at the extremities, about a
hundred and twenty feet tall at its
loftiest point, not more picturesque
than a rock covered with snow, and
interesting only to my mind because
of the distance it had measured, and
because of the fancies it raised in one
of the white, silent, and stirless prin-
cipalities from which it had floated
into these parts.

"Get the jolly-boat over, Mr.
Sweers," said the captain, "and take
a hand with you, and go and have a
look at that craft there; and if you
can board her, do so, and bring away
her log-book, if you come across it.
The newspapers sha' n't say that I
fell in with such an object as that and
passed on without taking any notice."

I caught Mr. Sweers' eye. "You 'll
do," said he, and in a few minutes he
and I were pulling away in the direction of the ice, I in the bow and he
aft, rowing fisherman fashion, face
forward. The schooner had backed
her yards on the fore when she was

within a mile of the berg, and we had
not far to row.   Our four arms made
the fat little jolly-boat buzz over the
wrinkled surface of the green, cold
water.   The wreck—if a wreck she
could be called—lay with her decks
sloping seawards upon an inclined
shelf or beach of ice, with a mass of
rugged, abrupt stuff behind her, and
vast coagulated lumps heaped like a
Stonehenge at her bows and at her
stern.   When we approached the
beach, as I may term it, Salamon
Sweers said :

"I'll tell you what : I am not
going to board that craft alone,
Kerry.   Who's to tell what's inside
of her?   She may have been lying
twenty years, for all we know,
frozen up where it's always day or
always night—where everything's
out of the order of nature, in fact;
and rat me if I'm going to be the
first man to enter her cabin."

"I'm along with you," said I.

"So you are, David," said he,
"and we'll overhaul her together,
and the best way to secure the boat'll
be to drag her high and dry"; and
as he said this, the stem of the boat
touched the ice, and we both of us
jumped out, and, catching hold of her
by the gunwale, walked her up the
slope by some five times her own

length, where she lay as snug as
though chocked aboard her own
mother, the schooner.

Sweers and I stood, first of all, to
take a view of the barque—for a
barque she was : her topgallant-
masts down, but her topsail and
lower yards across, sails bent, all
gear rove, and everything right so far
as we could see, saving that her flying
jib-boom was gone. There was no need
to look long at her to know that she
had n't been one of Franklin's ships.
Her name and the place she hailed
from were on her stern : the *President*, New Bedford. And now it was
easy to see that she was a Yankee
whaler. Her sides bristled with
cranes or davits for boats, but every
boat was gone. The tackles were
overhauled, and the blocks of two of
them lay upon the ice. She was a
stout, massive, round-bowed structure, to all appearances as sound as
on the day when she was launched.
She was coppered ; not a sheet of
metal was off, not a rent anywhere
visible through the length and breadth
of the dingy green surface of it.

We first of all walked round her,
not knowing but that on the other
side, concealed from the landing-
place by the interposition of the hull,
some remains of her people might be

lying ; but there was nothing in that
way to see.   We united our voices in
a loud "Hallo!" and the rocks re-
echoed us ; but all was still, frozen,
lifeless.

"Let 's get aboard," said Mr.
Sweers, gazing, nevertheless, up at
the ship's side with a flat face of re-
luctance and doubt.

I grasped a boat's fall and went
up hand over hand, and Sweers followed me.   The angle of the deck
was considerable, but owing to the
flat bilge of the whaler's bottom, not
greater than the inclination of the
deck of a ship under a heavy press
of canvas.   It was possible to walk.
We put our legs over the rail and
came to a stand, and took a view of
the decks of the ship.   Nothing, saving the boats, seemed to be missing.
Every detail of deck furniture was
as complete as though the ship were
ready for getting under way, with
a full hold, for a final start home.
Caboose, scuttle-butts, harness-cask,
wheel, binnacle, companion-cover,
skylight, winch, pumps, capstan—
nothing was wanting ; nothing but
boats and men.

"Is it possible that all hands can
be below ?" said Sweers, straining
his ear.

I looked aloft and about me, wondering that the body of the vessel and her masts and rigging should not be sheathed with ice ; but if ever the structure had been glazed in her time, when she lay hard and fast far to the north of Spitzbergen, for all one could tell, nothing was now frozen ; there was not so much as an icicle anywhere visible about her. The decks were dry, and on my kicking a coil of rope that was near my feet the stuff did not crackle, as one could have expected, as though frosted to the core.

"The vessel seems to have been thawed through," said I, "and I expect that this berg is only a fragment of the mass that broke adrift with her."

"Likely enough," said Sweers. "Hark ! what is that ?"

"What do you hear ?" I exclaimed.

"Why, *that!*" cried he, pointing to a shallow fissure in the icy rocks which towered above the ship : and down the fissure I spied a cascade of water falling like smoke, with a harsh, hissing noise, which I had mistaken for the seething of the sea. I ran my eye over the face of the heights and witnessed many similar falls of water.

"There'll not be much of this iceberg left soon," said I, "if the drift is to the southward."

" What d' ye think,—that the drift 's northerly?" exclaimed Sweers. " I 'll tell you what it is ; it 's these icebergs drifting in masses down south into the Atlantic which cause the sudden spells of cold weather you get in England during seasons when it ought to be hot."

As he said this he walked to the companion-hatch, the cover of which was closed, and the door shut. The cover yielded to a thrust of his hand. He then pulled open the doors and put his head in, and I heard him spit.

" There 's foul air here," said he ; " but where a match will burn a man can breathe, I 've learnt."

He struck a match, and descended two or three steps of the ladder, and then called out to me to follow. The air was not foul, but it was close, and there was a dampish smell upon it, and it was charged with a fishy odour like that of decaying spawn and dead marine vegetation. Light fell through the companion-way, and a sort of blurred dimness drained through the grimy skylight.

We thoroughly overhauled this interior, spending some time in looking about us, for Sweers' fear of beholding something affrighting vanished when he found himself in a plain ship's cabin, with nothing more

terrible to behold than the ship's
furniture of a whaleman's living-room
of near half a century old. There
were three sleeping-berths, and these
we explored, but met with nothing
that in any way hinted at the story of
the ship. It was impossible to tell,
indeed, which had been the captain's
cabin. All three berths were filled
alike with lockers, hammocks, wash-
stands, and so forth ; and two of
them were lighted by dirty little scuttles in the ship's side ; but the third
lay athwartships, and all the light
that it received came from the cabin
through its open door.

I don't know how long we were
occupied in hunting these cabins for
any sort of papers which would enable Captain Funnel to make out the
story of the barque. We were too
eager and curious and interested to
heed the passage of time. There
were harpoons and muskets racked in
the state cabin, some wearing apparel
in the berths, a few books on nautical
subjects, but without the owners'
names in them, and there was a bundle of what proved to be bear's skins
stowed away in the corner of the
berth that was without a scuttle. A
door led to a couple of bulk-headed
compartments in the fore part of the
state cabin, and Sweers was in the

act of advancing to it when he cried
out :

" By the tunder of heaven, what is
dot ? " losing his customary hold of
the English tongue in the excitement
of the moment.

" The ice is melting and discharg-
ing in Niagara Falls upon the whaler's
deck ! " I cried, after listening a moment to the noise of a downpour
that rang through the cabin in a hollow thunder.

We rushed on deck. A furious
squall was blowing, but the air was
becalmed where the vessel lay by the
high cliffs of ice, and the rain of the
squall fell almost up and down in a
very sheet of water, intermingled
with hailstones as big as the eggs of
a thrush. The whole scene of the
ocean was a swirling, revolving
smother, as though the sky was full
of steam, and the screech of the wind,
as it fled off the edge of the dead
white heights which sheltered us,
pierced the ear like the whistlings of
a thousand locomotives.

There was nothing to be seen of
the schooner : but *that* was trifling
for the moment compared to this :
*there was nothing to be seen of the
boat !* The furious discharge of the
squall would increase her weight by
half filling her with water ; the slash-

ing wet of the rain would also render the icy slope up which we had hauled her as slippery as a sheet for skaters ; a single shock or blast of wind might suffice to start her.   Be this as it will, she had launched herself—she was gone! We strained our sight, but no faintest blotch of shadow could we distinguish amid the white water rushing smoothly off from the base of the berg, and streaming into the pallid shadow of the squall where you saw the sea clear of the ice beginning to work with true Atlantic spite.

"Crate   Cott ! "   cried   Sweers, " what 's to be done ?   There was no appearance of a squall when we landed here.   It drove up abaft this berg, and it may have been hidden from the schooner herself by the ice."

We crouched in the companion-way for shelter, not doubting that the squall would speedily pass, and that the schooner, which we naturally supposed lay close to the berg hove-to, would, the instant the weather cleared, send a boat to take us off. But the squall, instead of abating, gradually rose into half a gale of wind—a wet dark gale that shrouded the sea with flying spume and rain to within a musket-shot of the iceberg, whilst the sky was no more than a weeping, pouring shadow coming and

going as it were with a lightening and
darkening of it by masses of headlong torn vapour. Some of the ragged pinnacles of the cliffs of ice
seemed to pierce that wild dark, flying sky of storm as it swept before
the gale close down over our heads.

We could not bring our minds to
realise that we were to be left aboard
this ice-stranded whaler all night, and
perhaps all next day, and for heaven
alone knows how much longer for
the matter of that ; and it was not
until the darkness of the evening had
drawn down, coming along early with
the howling gloom of the storm-
shrouded ocean, without so much as
a rusty tinge of hectic to tell us where
the West lay, that we abandoned our
idle task of staring at the sea, and
made up our minds to go through
with the night as best we could.

And first of all we entered the
galley, and by the aid of such dim
light as still lived we contrived to
catch sight of a tin lamp with a spout
to it dangling over the coppers.
There was a wick in the spout, but
one might swear that the lamp had n't
been used for months and months.

"We must have a light anyhow,"
said Sweers, "and if this *President*
be a whaler, there should be no lack
of oil aboard."

After groping awhile in some shelves stocked with black-handled knives and forks, tin dishes, pannikins, and the like, I put my hand upon a stump of candle-end. This we lighted, Sweers luckily having a box of lucifers in his pocket, and with the aid of the candle-flame, we discovered in the corner of the galley a lime-juice jar half-full of oil. With this we trimmed the lamp, and then stepped on deck to grope our way to the cabin, meaning to light the lamp down there, for no unsheltered flame would have lived an instant in the fierce draughts which rushed and eddied about the decks.

We stayed a moment to look seawards, but all was black night out there, touched in places with a sudden flash of foam. The voice of the gale was awful with the warring noise of the waters, and with the restless thunder of seas smiting the ice on the weather side, and with the wild and often terrific crackling sounds which arose out of the heart of the solid mass of the berg itself, as though earthquakes in endless processions were trembling through it, and as though, at any moment, the whole vast bulk would be rent into a thousand crystal splinters. Sweers was silent until we had gained the cabin and lighted

the lamp. He then looked at me
with an ashen face, and groaned.

"This gale's going to blow the
schooner away," said he. "We're
lost men, David. I'd give my right
eye to be aboard the *Lightning*. D'ye
understand the trick of these blooming icebergs? They wash away un-
derneath, grow topheavy, and then
over goes the show. And to think
of the jolly-boat making off, as if two
sailormen like you and me couldn't
have provided for *that!*"

He groaned again, and then seated
himself, and appeared wholly de-
prived of energy and spirit.

However, now that I was below,
under shelter, out of the noise of the
weather, and therefore able to collect
my thoughts, I began to feel very
hungry and thirsty; in fact, neither
Sweers nor I had tasted food since
breakfast at eight o'clock that morning. A lamp hung aslant from the
cabin ceiling. It was a small lamp
of brass, glazed. I unhooked it, and
brought it to the light, but it was
without a wick, and there was no oil
in it, and to save time I stuck the
lighted candle in the lamp, and leaving the other lamp burning to enable
Sweers to rummage also, I passed
through the door that was in the
forepart of the cabin; and here I

found three berths, one of which was furnished as a pantry, whilst the other two were sleeping-places, with bunks in them, and I observed also a sheaf or two of harpoons, together with spades and implements used in dealing with the whale after the monster has been killed and towed alongside.

The atmosphere was horribly close and fishy in this place, reeking of oil, yet cold as ice, as though the ship lay drowned a thousand fathoms deep. I called to Sweers to bring his lamp, for my candle gave so poor a light I could scarce see by it ; and in the berth that looked to have been used as a pantry we found half a barrel of pork, a bag of ship's biscuit, and a quantity of Indian meal, beans, and rice, a canister of coffee, and a few jars of pickles. But we could find nothing to drink.

I was now exceedingly thirsty ; so I took a pannikin—a number of vessels of the sort were on the shelf in the pantry—and carried it with the lamp on deck. I had taken notice during the day of four or five buckets in a row abaft the mainmast, and, approaching them, I held the light close, and found each bucket full. I tasted the water ; it was rain and without the least flavour of salt ; and, after drinking heartily, I filled the pannikin afresh and carried it down to Sweers.

There was a spiritlessness in this man that surprised me. I had not thought to find the faculties of Sala-mon Sweers so quickly benumbed by what was indeed a wild and danger-ous confrontment, yet not so formid-able and hopeless as to weaken the nerves of a seaman. I yearned for a bottle of rum, for any sort of strong waters indeed, guessing that a dram would help us both ; and after I had made a meal off some raw pork and molasses spread upon the ship's bis-cuit, which was mouldy and astir with weevils, I took my lantern and again went on deck, and made my way to the galley where the oil jar stood, and here in a drawer I found what now I most needed, but what before I had overlooked ; I mean a parcel of braided lamp wicks. I trimmed the lamp and got a brilliant light. The glass protected the flame from the rush of the wind about the deck. I guessed there would be nothing worth finding in the barque's fore-castle, and not doubting that there was a lazarette in which would be stored such ship provisions as the crew had left behind them, I re-turned to the cabin, looked for the lazarette hatch, and found it under the table.

Well, to cut this part of the story short, Sweers and I dropped into the lazarette, and after spending an hour or two in examining what we met with, we discovered enough provisions, along with some casks of rum and bottled beer, to last a ship's company of twenty men a whole six months. This was Sweers' reckoning. We carried some of the bottled beer into the cabin, and having pipes and tobacco with us in our pockets, we filled and smoked, and sat listening to the wet storming down the decks overhead, and to the roaring of the wind on high, and to the crackling noises of the ice.

That first night with us on board the whaler was a fearful time. Sometimes we dozed as we sat confronting each other on the lockers, but again and again would we start up and go on deck, but only to look into the blindness of the night, and only to hearken to the appalling noises of the weather and the ice. When day broke there was nothing in sight. It was blowing strong, a high sea was running, and the ocean lay shrouded as though with vapour.

During the course of the morning we entered the forepeak, where we

found a quantity of coal. This en-
abled us to light the galley fire, to
cook a piece of pork, and to boil
some coffee. Towards noon Sweers
proposed to inspect the hold, and to
see what was inside the ship. Accordingly we opened the main hatch
and found the vessel loaded with
casks, some of which we examined
and found them full of oil.

"By tunder!" cried Sweers; "if
we could only carry this vessel home
there 'd be a fortune for both of us,
David. Shall I tell you what this
sort of oil 's worth? Well, it 's worth
about thirty pounds a ton. And
how much d' ye think there 's
aboard? Not less than a hundred
ton, if I don't see double. There 's
no man can teach me the capacity of
a cask, and there are casks below
varying from forty-two to two hundred and seventy-five gallons, with no
lack of whalebone stored dry somewhere, I don't doubt, if those casks
would let us look for it."

But this was no better than idle
and ironical chatter in the mouths of
men so hideously situated as we were.
For my part I had no thought of
saving the ship; indeed, I had scarce
any hope of saving my own life. We
found an American ensign in a small
flag-locker that was lashed near the

wheel, and we sent it half-mast high, with the stars inverted. Then we searched for fresh water, and found three iron tanks nearly full in the after-hold. The water stunk with keeping, as though it had grown rank in the bilge, but after it had stood a little while exposed to air it became sweet enough to use. There was no fear then of our perishing from hunger and thirst whilst the whaler kept together. Our main and imminent danger lay in the sudden dissolution of the ice, or in the capsizal of the berg. It was our unhappy fortune that, numerous as were the cranes overhanging the whaler's side, we should not have found a boat left in one of them. Our only chance lay in a raft ; but both Sweers and I, as sailors, shrank from the thought of such a means of escape. We might well guess that a raft would but prolong our lives in the midst of so wide a sea, by a few days, and perhaps by a few hours only, after subjecting us to every agony of despair and of expectation, and torturing us with God alone would know what privations.

We thoroughly overhauled the forecastle of the vessel, but found nothing of interest. There were a few seamen's chests, some odds and ends of wearing apparel, and here

and there a blanket in a bunk ; but
the crew in clearing out appeared to
have carried off most of their effects
with them. Of course we could only
conjecture what they had done and
how they had managed ; but it was
to be guessed that all the boats being gone the sailors had taken advan-
tage of a split in the ice to get away
from their hard and fast ship, em-
ploying all their boats that they
might carry with them a plentiful
store of water and provisions.

I should but weary you to dwell
day by day upon the passage of time
that Sweers and I passed upon this
ship that we had seen upon the ice.
We kept an eager look-out for craft,
crawling to the mastheads so as to
obtain a view over the blocks of ice
which lay in masses at the stem and
stern of the whaler. But though we
often caught sight of a distant sail,
nothing ever approached us close
enough to observe our signal. Once,
indeed, a large steamer passed within a couple of miles of the iceberg,
and we watched her with devouring
eyes, forever imagining that she was
slowing down and about to stop, until she vanished out of our sight past
the north end of the berg. Yet, we
had no other hope of rescue than that
of being taken off by a passing ship.

I never recollect meeting at sea with such a variety of weather as we encountered. There would be clear sunshine and bright blue skies for a day, followed by dark and bellowing nights of storm. Then would come periods of thick fogs, followed by squalls, variable winds, and so on. We guessed, however, that our trend was steadily southwards, by the steady cascading of the ice, by the frequent falls of large blocks, and by the increasing noises of sudden, tremendous disruptions, loud and heart-subduing as thundershocks heard close to.

"If we are n't taken off," said Sweers to me one day, "there 's just this one chance for us. The ice is bound to melt. All these bergs, as I reckon, disappear somewhere to the nor'ard of the verge of the Gulf Stream. Well, now the Lord may be good to us, and it may happen that this berg 'll melt away and leave the whaler afloat ; and float she must if she is n't crushed by the ice. Let her leak like a sieve—there 's oil enough in her to keep her standing upright as though she were a line-of-battle ship."

Well, we had been a little more than a fortnight upon this ship hard and fast upon the ice. Many a ves-

sel had we sighted, but never a one
of them, saving the steamer I have
mentioned, had approached within
eyeshot of our distress signal. Yet
our health was good, and our spirits
tolerably easy; we had fared well,
there was no lack of food and drink,
and we were beginning to feel some
confidence in the iceberg—by which
I mean to say that the rapid thawing
of its upper parts, where all the
weight was, filled us with the hope
that the mass would n't capsize as we
had feared; that it would hold together so as to keep the ship on end
as she now was until we were rescued, or, failing our being rescued,
that it would dissolve in such a way
as to leave the whaler afloat.

It was somewhere about the end
of a fortnight, as I have said. My
bed was a cabin locker, on which I
had placed a mattress and a bear-
skin. Both Sweers and I turned in
of a night, unless it was clear
weather; though if I awoke I 'd
sometimes steal on deck to take a
peep, for nothing could come of our
keeping a look-out if it was blowing
hard, and if it was black and thick.

This night it was a bit muddy and
dark, with a moderate breeze out of
the south-west, as far as we could
guess at the bearings of the wind. I

was awakened from a deep slumber
by an extraordinary convulsion in
the ship. I was half-stupefied with
sleep, and can therefore but im-
perfectly recall my sensations and
the character of what I may term the
throes and spasms of the vessel. I
was thrown from the locker and lay
for some moments incapable of rising by the shock of the fall. But
one thing my senses, even when they
were scarce yet awake, took note of,
and that was a prodigious roaring
noise, similar in effect to what might
be produced by a cannon-ball rolling
along a hollow wooden floor, only
that the noise was thousands of
times greater than ever could have
been produced by a cannon-ball.
The lamp was out, and the cabin in
pitch blackness. I heard Sweers
from some corner of the cabin, bawling out my name ; but before I
could answer, and even whilst I was
staggering to my feet, a second convulsion threw me down again ; the
next instant there was a sensation
as of the vessel being hove up into
the air, attended by an extraordinary
grinding noise, that thrilled through
every beam of her ; next, in the space
of a few beats of the heart, she
plunged into the sea, raising such a
boiling and roaring of waters, as, spite

of the sounds being dulled to our
ears by our being in the cabin, per-
suaded us that the vessel was foun-
dering.

But even whilst I thus thought,
holding my breath and waiting for
the death that was to come with the
pouring of the water down the open
companion-way, I felt the ship right ;
she lifted buoyant under foot, and I
sprang to the steps which conducted
on deck, with Sweers—as I might
know by his voice—close at my heels,
roaring out, " By tunder, we 're adrift
and afloat ! "

The stars were shining, there was a
red moon low in the west, the weather
had cleared, and a quiet wind was
blowing. At the distance of some
hundred yards from the ship stood a
few pallid masses—the remains of the
berg. It was just possible to make
out that the water in the neighbourhood of those dim heaps was covered
with fragments of ice. How the
liberation of the ship had come about
neither Sweers nor I did then pause
to consider. We were sailors, and
our first business was to act as sailors,
and as quickly as might be we loosed
and hoisted the jib and foretopmast
staysail, so that the vessel might
blow away from the neighbourhood
of the dangerous remains of her jail

of ice. We then sounded the well, and, finding no water, went to work to loose the foresail and foretopsail, which canvas we made shift to set with the aid of the capstan. I then lighted the binnacle lamp whilst Sweers held the wheel ; and having sounded the well afresh, to make sure of the hull, we headed away to the eastwards, the wind being about W. S. W.

Before the dawn broke we had run the ice out of sight. Sweers and I managed, as I have no doubt, to arrive at the theory of the liberation of the ship by comparing our sensations and experiences. There can be no question that the berg had split in twain almost amidships. This was the cause of the tremendous noise of thunder which I heard. The splitting of the ice had hoisted the shelf or beach on which the barque lay, and occasioned that sensation of flying into the air which I had noticed. But the lifting of the beach of ice had also violently and sharply sloped it, and the barque, freeing herself, had fled down it broadside on, taking the water with a mighty souse and crash, then rising buoyant, and lifting and falling upon the seas as we had both of us felt her do.

And now to bring this queer yarn

to a close, for I have no space to
dwell upon our thankfulness and our
proceedings until we obtained the
help we stood in need of. We managed to handle the barque without
assistance for three days, then fell in
with an American ship bound to
Liverpool, who lent us three of her
men, and within three weeks of the
date of our release from the iceberg
we were in soundings in the Chops of
the Channel, and a few days later had
safely brought the barque to an
anchor in the river Thames.

The adventure yielded Sweers and
I a thousand pounds apiece as salvage
money, but we were kept waiting a
long time before receiving our just
reward. It was necessary to communicate with the owners of the
barque in America, and then the law-
yers got hold of the job, and I grew
so weary of interviews, so vexed and
sickened by needless correspondence,
that I should have been thankful to
have taken two hundred pounds for
my share merely to have made an
end.

It seems that the *President* had
been abandoned two years and five
months by her crew before the *Lightning* sighted her on the ice. Her
people had stuck to her for eight
months, then made off in a body with

the boats, carrying their captain and
mates along with them. They regarded the situation of their ship as
hopeless, and indeed, as it turned
out, they were not very wrong, so far
as their notions of reasonable deten-
tion went ; for they never could have
liberated the vessel by their own
efforts ; they must have waited, as we
had, for the ice to free her ; and this
would have signified to them an im-
prisonment of two years and a half
over and above the eight months
they had already spent in her whilst
ice-bound.

Sweers gave up the sea, started in
business, and died, about ten years
since, a fairly well-to-do man. And
shall I tell you what I did with my
thousand pounds ? . . . But my
story has already run to greater
length than I had intended when
sitting down to write it.

THE END.

THE INCOGNITO LIBRARY.

A series of small books by representative writers, whose names will for the present not be given.

In this series will be included the authorized American editions of the future issues of Mr. Unwin's " PSEUDONYM LIBRARY," which has won for itself a noteworthy prestige.

32mo, limp cloth, each 50 cents.

I. THE SHEN'S PIGTAIL, and Other Cues of Anglo-China Life, by Mr. M——.

II. THE HON. STANBURY AND OTHERS, by Two.

III. LESSER'S DAUGHTER, by Mrs. Andrew Dean.

IV. A HUSBAND OF NO IMPORTANCE, by " Rita."

V. HELEN, by Oswald Valentine.

VI. A GENDER IN SATIN, by " Rita."

VII. EVERY DAY'S NEWS, by C. E. Francis.

These will be followed by volumes by other well-known authors.